TAKING THE LEAD

Shelley had tried for months not to think about the Thompson climb, or any climbing expedition, for that matter. But Kevin had caught her completely by surprise, throwing open the floodgates of memory.

"Hey," Kevin said. "There's a climb in September. You'll be through here by then. Why don't you sign up?"

Shelley winced. He couldn't be teasing her, he was too nice for that.

"Really, why don't you?" Kevin prodded.

"I can't." Her words were just above a whisper.

She sensed Kevin turning on the sofa to look at her closely. "Why not?" he asked.

"What do you mean, why not? Do I have to spell it out to you?" Tears burned behind her eyelids. She fought to keep her voice from shaking. "It took me three days to learn my way around the Center—how do you think I'd make it on a rock climb?"

Bantam Sweet Dreams Romances
Ask your bookseller for the books you have missed

Sweet Dreams Specials

Taking the Lead
Deborah Kent

BANTAM BOOKS
TORONTO · NEW YORK · LONDON · SYDNEY · AUCKLAND

RL 6, IL age 11 and up

TAKING THE LEAD
A Bantam Book / June 1987

Taking the Lead

Chapter One

"Fold the road map, it keeps getting in the way," Mr. Sayer snapped, his voice tight with tension.

"I'm sorry, I thought you still wanted to look at it." Mrs. Sayer's voice fluttered above the crackle of paper, from the front seat. "I'll put it back in the glove compartment?" It was a question, not a statement. Lately, Shelley's mother never seemed sure enough of anything to come straight out and say it. It was always, "Nice day today, don't you think so?" or, "Those ceramic planters haven't turned over much in the shop since Christmas, have they?"

The glove compartment clicked shut, and no one said anything more. Maybe they could pick up something good on the car radio now that they were in Albuquerque—something with a beat that would bounce them all into a more cheerful frame of mind. But if Shelley suggested the radio, her mom would search all over the dial for just the right station,

1

desperate for Shelley to be pleased. It was better not to ask for anything, better just to keep her mouth shut.

The car slowed, probably bogging down in city traffic. They had left the mountains behind, winding down and down to the level of the city. Shelley huddled in her corner of the backseat, willing time to stand still. If she could only sit there forever, and never have to talk or move or even think again!

But her sister, Marge, wasn't one to leave a person in peace. "Shelley," she whispered, leaning across the canvas suitcase on the seat between them. "You want some M & M's?"

Shelley shook her head. How could Marge think about candy!

"Yes, this is Gonzalez Street!" Mrs. Sayer burst into another flurry or words. "There's the Exxon station; they said it'd be in the next block. Oh, it's a pretty place, Shelley! Colonial style, stone pillars, and Mexican tiles over the door. And they've got a couple of big old trees along this block. It'll be shady if you go out for a stroll—well, I mean, if . . ." She floated off into a cloud of uncertainty.

"I'll let you all out in front," Mr. Sayer announced. "Then I'll park and bring in the luggage. That way Shelley won't have so far to walk."

Suddenly there wasn't enough air in the car. Her family was so busy trying to protect her that Shelley might have suffocated, and not one of them would have noticed.

2

She didn't belong there! If it were a hospital, it would be different—some place where they knew more, where the techniques and equipment were completely up-to-date! But her parents couldn't deliver her there and leave her with a bunch of stumbling, groping strangers. Her parents had to know deep down that it was a terrible mistake.

"Come on, hon," her mom said brightly, opening the door. "Give me your hand."

For a moment longer Shelley clung to her corner. Nobody could make her move. She'd never get out, she'd never set foot in that lovely colonial-style dungeon with its pillars and tiles and shade trees.

Her mother's hand clasped hers and gave a faint tug. Shelley slid her free hand along the seat and caught the strap of her suede shoulder bag. She edged stiffly forward on the seat, extending a careful, searching foot.

"Watch out for the seat back," Mom exclaimed. "We ought to get a four-door car, it'd be so much easier getting in and out there! Don't trip on the curb! Step up! Fine!"

Maybe that was why she climbed out of the car at last. It cut off—for the moment—the worries and warnings that buzzed around her from the moment she awoke until she collapsed into bed again at night. She felt like a three-year-old, helplessly clutching her mother's hand as they slowly climbed up one, two, three steps. That suffocating feeling clutched at her again as her mother pushed a heavy door open and led her through it.

Her foot had just touched carpet when Marge spoke up behind her. "Southwest Regional Center for the Blind," she said deliberately, as though she were reading an inscription over the entrance.

For weeks everyone had been talking about The Center—her mom and dad, Dr. Rodriguez, and the social worker from the hospital up in Santa Fe. But no one had ever before dared to speak its name in full. Now Marge's voice cut through her like an icy knife. *Blind!* Center for the *Blind!* Such an ugly, condemning word, a word that couldn't have anything to do with Shelley Sayer. By mistake they had brought her here, by mistake they were leaving her in this place!

"Can I help you?" A woman's voice, brisk and efficient, came from straight ahead. "I'm Miss Chatham, the director. Do you want to register? Come over here, I'll help you fill out the forms."

Shelley tensed as her mother tried to back her into a chair. She didn't really sit down, she crumpled rather under the force of the voices that rattled around her. Let her mom fill out the forms. Let her dad carry the luggage. Let Marge read the name over the door. She didn't care. If she had to live like this for the rest of her life, she'd never care about anything again.

But Miss Chatham wouldn't leave her to herself. "Let's see now, you're fifteen, is that right?"

Shelley nodded.

"What year are you in?" Miss Chatham went on. "I mean, what grade will you enter in September?"

"I would have been a junior." Her own voice startled her. It sounded forced and mechanical, rusty from disuse.

Miss Chatham must have been too intent on her forms to notice. "Now, we've got your medical record, and the referral from your social worker. Looks like everything is in order. Would you like a tour of the facilities?"

"OK," Shelley said, but she didn't move until her mother took her hand again.

They trailed after Miss Chatham, their feet clattering down a long corridor. "The facilities!" Marge whispered. "Sounds like she's going to show us the washrooms or something!"

Shelley giggled with her sister. "The facilities!" she repeated. "Sure, let's go see the facilities!"

"Girls, really!" their mother said in a quick, taut voice. It all rushed back to her again—where she was, what had happened. How could she have put it out of her mind, even for a moment? Sure, Marge could make jokes. She was only eleven, and she was always off in her own world anyway. But there could never be anything funny about the Center for the Blind.

"This is the recreation-room," Miss Chatham announced. "When you come in the front door, you turn left and it's at the end of the hall. There's a long couch opposite the doorway, and there are several more chairs on either side of that. Now, off to the right, past the chairs, you've got a table where some of the trainees like to read or play games."

"Games?" Shelley heard herself repeat, bewildered. What sort of games could they play there? Nobody'd be able to read a deck of cards or a Scrabble board.

"Chess, Monopoly, Scrabble, you name it," Miss Chatham said, laughing. "There are all kinds of Braille games. Now, you're still facing into the room from the doorway, right? Over on your left, there are shelves with some Braille magazines and two listening booths. We've got cassette players with earphones so you can read talking books. And I almost forgot—at the far right we have a piano. Do you play?"

"No," Shelley muttered. Not yet, she thought ironically. But blind people were supposed to be musical, weren't they? Maybe blindness offered a hidden bonus. Maybe, for the first time in her life, she'd learn to carry a tune.

They turned down another corridor that led to what Miss Chatham called the model kitchen. "There are three sinks and two stoves, and there's a long L-shaped counter that begins on your right," she explained. "All of the trainees have cooking instruction, as well as work in the home repair department. You never know when you might have to change a washer, right?"

The whole idea was so preposterous, it was comical, in a grim sort of way. She could just

imagine a crew of blind people trying to prepare spaghetti and meatballs, bumping into
one another, knocking over open cans of tomato sauce, adorning the counters, walls, and
ceiling with chopped onions and ground meat.
But Miss Chatham went on matter-of-factly.

"Picture the whole building as a horseshoe.
There's a nice patio in the middle where you
can sit and get some fresh air. Down this last
corridor are the classrooms and offices. And
that's really it. Come into my office, and we'll
talk for a few minutes before I show you up-
stairs to your room."

As they entered Miss Chatham's office, Shelley banged her shin against a chair. Her mother's fingers immediately tightened on her arm.
"Oh, I'm sorry, Shel, I've got to learn to be
more careful," she exclaimed. "I forget sometimes—"

"I'm OK," Shelley muttered as she sat down.
She didn't mind bruising her shin nearly so
much as she minded hearing her mother apologize again and again.

"Let's see." Miss Chatham riffled through
some papers on her desk. "You're the youn-
gest trainee we have in this group."

"They told us all about you people up at the
hospital in Santa Fe," her dad said abruptly.
He must have joined them during the tour,
but he hadn't spoken since they arrived. "The
social worker there said you're the best in the
region. But to tell you the truth, I still think
this is a little premature. I'm from the East,
and I know they perform miracles at Mass

Eye and Ear. I just wonder if the doctors out here really know everything they should about glaucoma."

Hope sprang to life inside Shelley's chest, beating its wings like a wild bird. They wouldn't make her stay there. They'd go out to Boston; they'd find the right doctor, and he would perform the operation they had told her in Santa Fe couldn't be done. And suddenly she'd have it all back: faces, sunlight, books, pictures on the wall. She'd run fast down the road, not hanging on to anybody's hand. And she'd go mountain climbing again, she'd drink in the view as she never had before. . . .

"I can certainly understand your wanting to try every alternative." Miss Chatham's voice had turned suddenly formal, pushing her listeners to arm's length. In another moment she'd begin the same lecture they had all heard a half dozen times before. Shelley's family would be wasting their time and money on a trip to the East, building a lot of false hopes only to face a more crushing disappointment in the end. Shelley was *blind*: she might as well accept it and start learning how to live without her eyes.

She couldn't bear to listen to it again. And she didn't want her dad or mom or Marge to have to sit through it again, either. Marge would start kicking the leg of her chair, and her mom and dad would wrestle with their decision all over again under a fresh barrage of good, reasonable advice. Their lives had come to a standstill as they searched for a miracle after the operation failed. Somewhere within herself she knew that a trip to Boston wouldn't be any different from their visit to the eye hospital in Denver or the place in Phoenix: more waiting, more examinations, and the same verdict in the end.

Slowly, her mind made up, she turned toward her father. She sat up straight and tried to sound braver than she felt. "Well, I'm here now. I guess I may as well see if they can teach me anything."

"Nobody will tell you it's going to be easy." Warmth crept back into Miss Chatham's voice, pulling in her audience once again. Shelley wondered how many trembling newcomers had heard this speech before her. "You're going through a very trying adjustment right now. You probably still can't quite believe this has really happened to you. But it gets easier as time goes on. We'll work on all the ADL—that means activities of daily living—and in a couple of months you'll be on your own again."

What did Miss Chatham know about it? She sat behind a desk, leafing through her folder, reading one printed page after another. She could talk all she wanted about trying adjustments and ADL.

The silence lengthened, and she felt them all waiting for her to reply. "Will they teach me some way to figure out my clothes?" she asked finally. "You know, like how to tell what goes with what?"

"Grooming is part of the program," Miss

Chatham assured her. "And cooking, house-keeping, touch typing, Braille, listening skills, mobility—that's using a white cane. We'll keep you pretty busy."

"You think I'll learn all that in just eight weeks?"

"You'll be amazed once you start," Miss Chatham promised. Her chair creaked as she leaned forward. "You know, you could go down to the School for the Blind in Alamogordo for a year. But if you really work here, you might be ready to go back to your old school in September."

For just an instant that wild bird in her burst into life again. Her mother and father had hinted about the school in Alamogordo—without ever calling it the School for the Blind. But, perhaps, she wouldn't have to go there after all. She might go back to high school in Santa Fe, back to Lorna and Melissa and riding together on the schoolbus, back to literature class and math and greasy cafeteria food, back to Saturday night dates with Dave or Tom or Steven . . .

Suddenly Shelley couldn't catch her breath. "No!" she gasped. "I can't! How could I study? And get to my classes? And—and everything!" It hurt too much, thinking of it all and knowing that it would never be the same again. Her eyes burned. They were no longer good for telling red from green, they couldn't show her the way to "the facilities" in a strange building, but they definitely hadn't forgotten how to produce tears.

She covered her face with her hands and tried to pretend she was stifling a sneeze. In a moment she had control of herself again. Miss Chatham was talking, her tone soft and confidential. "Don't think that far ahead, dear. Just take it one step at a time. First thing on your agenda this afternoon is going up to your room."

The casters squeaked as she pushed her chair back and stood up. "Lets' see, you're in room two-oh-five. You want to take my arm and I'll show you?"

Shelley tentatively reached out and found the arm Miss Chatham was offering. It was covered in light cottony fabric—a long-sleeved blouse or dress. She'd never get used to not knowing what people wore or what they looked like. All the time they talked her mind had been conjuring up an image of Miss Chatham. In Shelley's imagination, Miss Chatham was short and dumpy, and her dowdy clothes made her look like someone's great-aunt. She was wearing too much powder, so she had dusty splotches next to her nose. Standing beside her, however, Shelley realized Miss Chatham was taller than she had imagined. The rest of the picture might have been completely wrong, too.

"If you hold my arm and follow me, you can sense when I turn corners or pause for steps," Miss Chatham explained. "If I take your arm and push you ahead of me, you won't know what's coming."

Shelleys' parents usually pushed her from

place to place, propelling her through swinging doors and up and down curbs, their tension quivering through the fingers that gripped her elbow. Now, with her hand tucked in the crook of Miss Chatham's arm, she moved almost easily along the hallway. The others followed behind them, and she realized with surprise that they were walking at a nearly normal pace.

"Well," Miss Chatham said brightly when they arrived at room 205. "I see two suitcases by the far bed. Looks like your roommate's here already."

"My roommate?" Shelley repeated. In her grimmest imaginings about the Center for the Blind, it had never occurred to her that she wouldn't have a room to herself.

"Yes, you'll be sharing with Angela Sollano," Miss Chatham explained. "She's eighteen. The two of you are our only teenagers this session."

The only teenagers! Miss Chatham made it sound like something to be proud of. After all, blindness usually went along with wrinkles and dentures. How precocious of her, to have reached that state at such an early age! Shelley gripped the back of her chair, stifling a wild urge to run back down the long, cold corridor. She didn't belong there.

But where *did* she belong? She couldn't picture herself back at school with the friends she had known most of her life and the boys who used to ask her to the movies. And the Climbing Club no longer had a place for her, either. Never again would she know the exhilaration of standing on a snowy peak with the whole world shimmering far below her. She positively couldn't go home to sit again day after day in front of the babbling TV, her mom scurrying to and fro with glasses of lemonade and empty snippets of talk about her souvenir shop and the neighbors and tourists. If Shelley wanted to hang on to her sanity, she couldn't let herself belong there, either.

Miss Chatham left to show someone else around, and her mother and Marge helped Shelley unpack. By the time her father announced that they had better head back to Santa Fe, she could hear other arrivals settling in up and down the hall. Keys jingled, doors slammed, suitcases thumped to the floor, voices rose and fell. Slow, heavy footsteps shuffled past the open door. With a sinking in her stomach, Shelley knew that her own groping steps must sound the same way.

The goodbyes were hasty—a quick hug and a peck on the cheek from her mother and her father's brusque assurance from the doorway: "It'll turn out fine, Shel, just give it a little time."

"I will," Shelley said, and she thought she had found a spark of courage. But after she had hugged Marge goodbye and listened as her family's steps faded, she sank onto the bed, her face buried in her hands, too miserable for tears. It wasn't even that bad at the hospital in Santa Fe where they took her for the emergency eye surgery that hadn't helped at all. Her parents were there when she awoke, explaining even before she was fully conscious that they'd find another doctor, they wouldn't give up. But they *had* given up. They had dumped her with a bunch of blind people and dashed back to their own lives.

Chapter Two

"Hey, anybody here yet?"

The door banged back against the wall, and Shelley leaped up as someone stepped down heavily on her left foot. "Yes, I'm here," she said. "You're my roommate?"

"If this is room two-oh-five I am." Without apologizing for crushing Shelley's toes or waiting for an invitation, the stranger flopped down onto the end of the bed, and Shelley heard two light taps as she kicked off a pair of shoes.

"That's the number the director told me," Shelley said. "I guess you're Angela Sollano."

"Angela!" the girl said with derision. "I'm no angel. My friends all call me Bette."

"How come? I mean, if Angela's your name—"

"Maria started it when I was fifteen. She's this crazy friend of mine. One night she just decided I looked like a Bette—she spelled it like Bette Midler, you know? And I thought, hey, I *feel* like a Bette, too."

She had bumped into the door and stepped

on Shelley's foot. But could Bette really be blind and still chatter away as if her life had no snags?

"Who sent you here?" Shelley asked. "Did some social worker talk your parents into it, too?"

"Social worker!" Bette repeated, with the same derision she had assigned to her real name. "I don't talk to those people! It was my grandmother. She found this place in the Yellow Pages, can you believe it? She figures maybe they'll teach me to type or something useful like that."

"You make it sound like this is a boarding school or something," Shelley remarked.

Bette sighed. "Don't I wish! You wait, they'll have more stupid rules here than any boarding school could dream up in forty years."

By now Shelley's curiosity had the upper hand. "How long has it been—since you could see?"

Bette's tone was matter-of-fact. "Three years—no, almost four now. I got some sort of virus. There's this fancy name for it, but I never can remember it."

"You've been blind for almost four years?" Shelley said in awe. "How do you stand it?"

The bedsprings shifted as Bette stood up. She padded surely across to her own side of the room before she replied. "You're not going to be one of *those*, are you?" She filled her voice with enough melodrama for an afternoon soap opera and lamented, "What shall I

.do! I'm lost in a world of darkness! How will I ever find my toothbrush?"

"Well, it is terrible," Shelley said, trying to defend herself. "I mean, I never was exactly an angel, either, but I didn't do anything bad enough to deserve this."

"Who said anything about deserving!" Bette said scornfully. "It's just a roll of the dice. That's the way I figure it."

Shelley was only half listening. "I should have been prepared, I guess," she said, running her fingers over the ridged bedspread. "They found out I had glaucoma when I was a little kid. I always had to put drops in my eyes every night. And one time I heard the doctor say something to my mother about finding a training program if the worst came to the worst—"

"As soon as you get blind, everybody wants to *train* you," Bette observed. "When I could see, I just hung out and nobody worried about me."

Somewhere in the corridor a bell jangled, one long ring like the bell that signaled the end of class back in Shelley's school. "Dinner in ten minutes," called Miss Chatham from the hallway. "We expect all you ladies to be on time."

"Where'd I leave my sandals?" Bette muttered, thumping down on her hands and knees.

Shelley slid to the end of the bed and found a loose shoe with her outstretched foot. "Over here. You took them off when you came in."

For months she had scarcely been able to keep track of her own belongings. She was forever hollering for someone to help her find her sweater or her comb or her other earring.

Now she held the sandals out and waited. Bette's searching hand grazed her wrist, and at last she took the shoes Shelley was trying to give her.

There was no doubt about it. Bette really was blind, too. "Come on," she urged Shelley from the doorway. "Let's see what kind of meals we've got to put up with for the next eight weeks."

"Don't you think we had better wait? Somebody'll come and take us to the dining room, won't they?"

Bette paused. "They might," she said. "Or they might not."

Shelley sat motionless as the *slap-slap* of Bette's sandals receded down the hall. Then she sprang up and half stumbled for the door. "Wait up!" she cried. "I'm coming."

Up and down the hall other doors opened. Someone, walking slowly ahead of them, tapped a cane or stick along the floor, and behind them two women shuffled, their voices as cautious as their steps. "I wonder if they've got many partials here," Bette whispered.

"What are partials?"

"You know, people that have partial sight. There were a couple of them at this workshop they stuck me in making circuit cards. Watch out for them, some of them really try to lord it over you."

"If they can see, why'd they be here?"

"They can't see all that well. They're just partials."

They reached the end of the hall. Shelley hesitated. Miss Chatham had shown her the dining room, but she couldn't begin to remember where it was. "Down this way," Bette said, turning left. "You can hear knives and forks clanking around. Hey, I wonder if any of the guys'll be halfway decent?"

Shelley didn't answer. It was all she could do to set one foot in front of the other. At any instant the floor might yawn open and she would plunge down a flight of stairs. Or a stack of furniture could loom up out of nowhere before her, to topple over on her with a hideous crash. There was no room in her mind for boys anymore. How could anyone want her like this, anyway, fumbling and lost and having to have her meat cut up for her at the table? It was safer not to think about boys.

Miss Chatham stood in the doorway, directing traffic. Someone offered Shelley an arm and led her to a table. After a few moments she ventured to explore the space in front of her with a tentative hand and discovered a bowl too cool to be soup. She gingerly touched the contents, hoping no one witnessed her bad manners. Lettuce salad. She waited patiently, but nobody arrived to cut it up for her.

Across the table, a man cleared his throat.

19

"Hi," came his gruff voice. "Anybody know what's going on here? Are we supposed to dig in, or do we wait for some kind of go-ahead?"

"I'm starting," said Bette down at the far end. "I even found the salad dressing. Anybody want some?"

Before anyone could reply, a bell tinkled and Miss Chatham called for attention. "I'd like to take this opportunity to welcome all of you to the Southwest Regional Center for the Blind," she said. "Let me tell you a little bit about our program. Our purpose here is rehabilitation. That means training you to be as independent as you possibly can be. If you have some vision, you'll learn to use it to your best advantage. If you're totally blind, you'll find there are ways to do virtually everything you have to do without any sight at all."

She paused to let her words sink in. "Probably most of you have been getting a bit of coddling at home. But don't expect to be babied around here. It may take some getting used to at first, but you'll realize it's the only way you can learn."

"I think this would be a good time for us all to introduce ourselves," Miss Chatham went on. "I'm Miss Chatham. If you don't recognize my voice by now you will soon enough. I'm here and there and everywhere all day long. Mr. Donaldson, would you explain what you do?"

"I'm your mobility instructor. I'll be teaching you cane travel, crossing streets, taking buses, finding your way in stores." There was a hesitant quality to his voice, Shelley thought, as if he were nervous speaking to a group.

One by one the other teachers identified themselves. There was Mrs. Pardo, in charge of home ec, and Mr. Doyle, from the home repair shop. There was Ms. McDougal, who taught grooming, and Miss Flores, who taught typing, and there was the Braille instructor who simply called herself Pat.

Then it was the trainees' turn. One by one, from up and down two long tables, they introduced themselves. Most merely offered their names and hometowns, but a few referred to work they had done before their vision problems set in, or the things they hoped to master there at the center. There was Louise, a grandmother from Flagstaff, Arizona; there was Marco from the Zuni reservation; there was Ed, an engineering student who'd lost his sight in a car accident and still wanted to get his degree. By the time Shelley counted sixteen people, their names and voices were a meaningless blur.

"We'll be coming around to help serve your dinner tonight," Miss Chatham announced. "Mealtime is part of your learning experience, so we'll give you a few pointers along the way."

Mercifully, the lettuce and tomatoes in the salad in front of Shelley were in fairly small pieces, and she found it wasn't hard to manage them after all.

"Here's your dinner, Shelley," Miss Chatham eventually said at her elbow. A faint haze of steam still rose from the plate she had set before her. "Does anyone at this table know about eating by the clock?"

"Is that for real?" demanded Eddie. "It was in this book I read when I was a kid."

"It's definitely for real," Miss Chatham said. "Think of your plate as the face of a clock. Then if I say, for instance, 'Shelley, your potato is at twelve o'clock,' where will you find it?"

Shelley raised her fork and touched something round and solid at the top of her plate.

"That's it," Miss Chatham said. "Now, your chicken is at three—over on the right. Spinach is at six, and at nine you've got corn."

She moved on down the table. Shelley ate in silence, listening to the muted conversations all around her. The talk was all about the correct way to butter a roll, how to spoon gravy onto a potato, how to run a hand along the tablecloth and locate a glass of milk without knocking it over. She had to learn all these things, Shelley reminded herself. She couldn't go through life with her mother standing over her helping her eat. But there was something strange, almost bizarre about the whole meal. It was almost as if she were only dreaming that she was there, surrounded by fifteen other people who all ate dinner from the face of the clock.

At last the trainees were dismissed from dinner, and Shelley and Bette straggled after the others down to the lounge. "There's room on the couch, ladies," a man said as they enterd. "Over on your left."

"I'm not too good at voices yet," Shelley said apologetically, sitting down. "You must have said your name before, but I don't remember." Before he could enlighten her, she rushed on, "How did you know there was room on the couch? Are you a teacher?"

The man gave a rich, deep chuckle. "Not a chance. I'm a trainee, too. Isn't that what they keep calling us? Howard Burns."

"I'm Louise." From a chair to the right came a voice with a quaver of old age.

Howard must have been one of the partials Bette warned her about. He and Louise exchanged bits of personal data. She was a widow with four grandchildren and another one on the way. She had once sung in nightclubs, but that was more years ago than she wanted to count. Howard explained that he was a cabinetmaker who wanted to learn some new ways to work with tools before his sight was gone completely. He was married, he said, and had two boys right there in Albuquerque.

Bette was engrossed in a giggling conversation with Eddie, the engineering student, by the time Howard turned back to Shelley. "Where are you from?" he asked.

"Santa Fe." In consternation she discovered a large damp spot on her right sleeve where something must have splattered. She tried vainly to cover it with one hand. Then she smiled to herself. She was in a roomful of blind people—no one was going to notice. But how many people there could see as well as Howard did?

"You go to high school?" Howard inquired.

"Yeah. I was a sophomore this past year."

"Just a year behind my son Kevin, then. I'll introduce you one of these days."

Bette's voice, ringing with indignation, cut across the small talk. "There I was, just minding my own business, and she comes over and says, 'That's your dessert fork, Angela. You have to use the proper utensils.' "

"Who does she think she is—Emily Post?" Eddie grumbled. "Who cares what fork you use, as long as it gets the food into your mouth?"

"I think they want us to learn to do everything very correctly," Louise suggested. "When we leave here, you know, people will always be looking at us. We'll have to prove what we can do."

"You've got a point," Howard said. "If you can't see or can't hear or whatever, people tend to be sort of critical. They don't expect you to be able to do anything at all—or else they think you're some kind of superman."

"It's worse when you've got partial sight." Shelley couldn't pin a name to the hearty male voice that broke in from across the room. "A couple of weeks ago a lady started yelling at me for faking. I can still read really large print, and I was standing by a newsstand reading the headlines. I had my white cane in my hand."

Howard laughed. "I guess I'll have to start using one of those gadgets at night," he admitted. "You hate to give in to it, you know what I mean?"

"I finally got a cane a couple of months ago," Louise said. "I stepped on something soft and furry in the middle of the living room, and I about jumped out of my skin. Screamed so loud it brought my neighbor running. I was that sure the cat had brought in a poor baby rabbit. Turned out it was the wool sweater I'd been looking for all morning."

She chuckled, and to Shelley's amazement Bette and Eddie laughed, too. What was funny about an elderly blind woman, all alone, screaming in fright?

"You've got to keep your sense of humor about some of the things that happen," Howard said. "Some of it's pretty comical if you look at it in the right way."

"I was out shopping with my mother last week," Shelley said, startling herself. "The most embarrassing thing happened. I bumped into somebody and I said excuse me, and the person didn't answer. And then my mother said there wasn't anybody there—it was just a coat hanging on the rack!" She laughed a little unevenly, trying it out, like an experiment. "I guess even Miss Chatham might say that's carrying etiquette to an extreme."

They all laughed then, and with a rush of warmth she knew they were laughing with her. Because of their own mistakes and embarrassments, they all understood hers.

Perhaps eight weeks wouldn't be such an impossibly long time after all. Sitting there with that mismatched collection of strangers, Shelley felt for the first time in months that she was no longer all alone.

Chapter Three

"Right foot forward, tap your cane on the left side. Left foot forward, tap on the right side," Mr. Donaldson reminded her for the third time in ten minutes. "You've got to catch onto the natural rhythm."

"What's natural about tapping along with a stick?" Shelley grumbled. "I feel ridiculous!"

Already, in her first mobility lesson, she had discovered one thing about Mr. Donaldson. He didn't argue or even discuss. He simply waited her out, giving her the very deflating impression that he had heard it all before.

"Ready to give it another try?" he asked. Somehow they had gotten all the way down the corridor to the carpeted foyer.

"OK," Shelley said, straightening her shoulders. She got a firmer hold on the rubber grip at the top of the long, slender metal cane and held it out before her, her right arm fully extended the way Mr. Donaldson had shown her. She turned around to head back the way they had come and took the first tentative steps. Right, left, right, left, right. There was a jarring clang as the cane struck something solid. Shelley jolted to a stop.

"What was that?" she demanded.

"Why don't you tell me?" Mr. Donaldson's cool, level tone was infuriating. Shelley wondered if any of his trainees had ever used a cane to crack him over the head.

"A chair?" she suggested, trying to sound as unconcerned as Mr. Donaldson. She stepped closer and bent over to find out for certain. "No, the main desk. I should have known, there's the phone ringing."

"All right, if that's the main desk, which way do you go to get back into the corridor?"

Shelley stood still and thought. Behind her the front door swished open, letting in a puff of heat and the murmur of traffic. Ahead and to the left, heels clicked along a bare floor. "That way," she said, pointing. "The lounge is down at the end, right?"

Mr. Donaldson didn't believe in giving anything away. "Let's go find out," he said.

He walked beside her, slowing his pace to match hers as she stepped off the carpet, turned left, and made her way back along the echoing hall. Voices from the lounge assured her she was on the right track. She recognized Howard's tone of authority as he called out, "A little farther, Louise," and a gust of laughter from Bette. Shelley quickened her steps.

"The lounge." She turned to Mr. Donaldson in quiet triumph, her left hand on the wooden door frame. She couldn't help adding, "I told you so."

"You see? You're getting the hang of it," Mr. Donaldson said cheerfully. "Turn around and we'll go back to the main desk once more."

Tap left, tap right, tap left . . . She was walking faster now. The long hall was familiar after several journeys up and back. She knew for a fact that it was clear of furniture and concealed no gaping stairways. And even if there was an obstacle looming, she reminded herself, she'd find it with the cane before she banged into it, the way she had found the desk in the lobby.

"We could call it a day," Mr. Donaldson said when they stood on the carpet again. Shelley was about to agree when he added, "Or you could try something a little more interesting. How about a walk outside down to the corner?"

An hour earlier she would have objected. She already had collected enough new experiences for one day—chopping onions in the kitchen that morning, cutting up her own roast beef sandwich at lunch. But she hadn't severed any fingers, she hadn't dumped gravy onto her lap, and now she had found the lounge without any help at all. Her latest accomplishment filled her with energy.

"Sure," she said. "Why not?"

As Shelley stepped out into the seething heat of the July afternoon, she almost regretted her decision. Santa Fe, perched in the foothills of the Sangre de Cristo Mountains, was never hot like that. There in Albuquerque, down on the plains, the heat rolled in from the desert, driving people indoors to the artificial shade of air-conditioning. But she forgot about the heat as soon as she took her first tentative steps along the sidewalk. Her ears were straining to catch every sound that might give her a hint about the scene around her, and her whole body was braced to react to any warning the cane might send. Gonzalez was a quiet side street. Trees rustled overhead as a hot dry breeze spattered her face with dust. A car swept past, rock music blaring through its open windows. With each step she took, the cane promised that the pavement before her was solid and clear.

And then, just as she was beginning to relax, the tip of her cane plunged over a precipice. Her legs froze, her body went rigid with tension. "What happened?" she asked.

At least that time Mr. Donaldson didn't keep the answer a secret. "You've been veering to the left little by little. The top of your cane just slipped over the curb."

"I'll never learn to do this," Shelley moaned. "Maybe I'd better get a Seeing Eye dog."

"You'll never have to learn to use a cane if you get a dog, but a dog means other responsibilities," Donaldson said. "Besides, most of the guide-dog schools would rather you waited till you're out of high school. They don't want other kids feeding the dog at the table and petting it when it's working and things like that. Don't give up on the cane yet. You just got started."

"I thought I was going straight. I mean, how am I supposed to know?"

Mr. Donaldson came and stood beside her. Gently but firmly he grasped her wrist, swinging the cane before her in a low, narrow arc. "You've got to keep your arm centered," he explained. "If you tap too much over on the right, you tend to veer left."

Her shoulders sagged. It was so complicated.

"Take three steps to your right, and you'll be in the middle of the sidewalk," Mr. Donaldson said. "There's a mailbox on the corner, see if you can find it."

Once again she set off, concentrating on the position of her right arm and the cane's steady rhythm. She must have looked like a toddler, stumbling down the street with absurd little baby steps. She was no longer the person who had once climbed over snow-covered rocks to the summit of Thompson Mountain.

Shelley shook her head, pushing the memory aside. Right, left, right, left. Traffic roared up ahead, the noise drawing closer and closer with each step. Center Street was a busy main street. Howard had joked the night before that crossing it would be their final exam. She was barely inching along now, forcing herself forward against all her instincts. She wanted to keep her distance from those rumbling cars and trucks. Suppose the cane didn't warn her in time and she tripped over the curb, sprawling right in front of a speeding bus?

"About two more steps," Mr. Donaldson said gently. "There, you've got it."

Again the end of her cane dropped down into the street. Shelley reached out with her right foot and found the curb. She stood poised at the brink of the rushing river of traffic.

"Don't forget the mailbox." Mr. Donaldson refused to let her relax.

Shelley hesitated, trying to reason it out. Half turning, she searched with her cane over the empty pavement to her right. But somehow, she wasn't quite certain why, she sensed something off to her left. Bette had tried to explain how after a while she'd learn to feel the nearness of large objects—walls, parked cars, even people—and the echoes that bounced against them. She hadn't believed it, but maybe it was true after all.

She stretched out her hand, and there it was—the astonishing, unmistakable curve of an ordinary metal mailbox.

"Now if you want to write a letter to your boyfriend back home," Mr. Donaldson said jovially, "you'll know where to go and send it."

Shelley winced. Once she would have tossed back, "Which boyfriend?" And she would have meant it, too. There had been David with the crazy practical jokes, and Tom the sophomore class vice-president, and Rick the basketball center. She had liked all of them, and she had never doubted for an instant that they had liked her, too. She had plenty of girlfriends, she would argue. So what was wrong with being friends with more than one boy?

She pretended she hadn't heard Mr. Donaldson. He might know all about tapping a cane, but he sure didn't understand anything else in her life. She hadn't figured out much about him yet, except that he was unusually short for a man, probably not much taller than her own five-foot-six. And he was old—he seemed at least as old as her father.

"That was great for your first day out." Mr. Donaldson congratulated Shelley when they were back at the front door of the center. "We'll work for an hour every day this week. Next week we can take some longer trips."

"OK," she said, but her voice was flat. The triumphs had dissolved in the afternoon heat. She had been all right—even excited and happy at moments—as long as she didn't have to think about everything she had lost and everything she had to go back to when her eight-week training session came to an end. Now she felt completely deflated again. So what if she could cut up a sandwich or walk to a mailbox? Any sighted person could do those things without thinking.

Someone had switched on the TV in the lounge. Shelley searched for an empty chair, propped her cane against a table beside her, and tried to listen to the evening news. Another hijacking, a forest fire in California, a scandal about a state senator. None of it had anything to do with her.

Suppose she *could* write a letter somehow, suppose she could still trust her hand to control a pen and produce legible script: would

David or Tom or Rick want to hear from her now? Her friends had swamped her with visits in the beginning, of course. When she was in the hospital, the nurses had teased her about papering the walls with get-well cards. Melissa brought a mystery to read to her, but so many people kept dropping in that they didn't even finish the second chapter. And once Tom managed to sneak in after visiting hours to bring her a single long-stemmed rose in a tall fluted vase.

Then one afternoon David said that she had excellent timing, that she had staged the whole thing to get out of exams. "Hey, that's not funny, big mouth," Lorna exclaimed, and Shelley heard her lecturing him in a frantic whisper, though she couldn't catch any of the words. It was the first time any of the kids seemed to recognize that she wasn't going to get well, in spite of the fluffy good wishes in all those cards people kept reading to her.

She didn't get so many visits after she went home. Melissa still dropped by a lot, but her visits grew shorter and shorter. Shelley was too depressed to care about the mystery novel, and by chapter four they gave it up. They would sit on the patio, struggling to think of things to say, but there just wasn't anything left that was easy to talk about. Lorna only came once before she got busy with a job at Woolworth's. David and Rick each called once or twice, but after that she didn't hear from either of them anymore.

At least Tom had kept in touch. He called

her every few days, chatting about the crazy math substitute who kept talking about her canary or the futility of the sophomore class magazine sale.

But how could she expect Tom or anybody else to want to keep spending time with her now? They couldn't go out on normal dates, and she couldn't expect him to be satisfied just to sit and talk. No matter how smoothly she managed to walk with her cane, no matter how many onions she chopped, she would never be able to pretend nothing had changed. She could never tell when she might spill something or bang into someone or start talking to somebody who had just gotten up and walked away.

Bette's loud laughter brought her into the conversation around her. "So Maria drops me off, see, and she tells me it's the right house," Bette was saying above the jangle of a detergent commercial. "And Judy had said on the phone they wouldn't be home till late, but I could let myself in. She said the key's under the mat, right?"

"Everybody's key's under the mat, isn't it?" Eddie asked.

"What did I know?" Bette said. "I felt around and there was the key, so I open the door and sit down on the sofa to wait. So I'm sitting there, getting bored, thinking what the heck is keeping everybody—and all of a sudden I hear this real foghorn of a snore!"

The crowd laughed softly in anticipation.

"That nut Maria, she let me out in front of

the wrong house!" Bette shrieked through her laughter. "I could have died, no lie! Can you imagine? What if I'd decided to go find the kitchen and raid the fridge!"

"What in the world did you do?" Shelley asked in horror.

Before Bette could explain, hurried steps crossed the lounge, and Miss Chatham called, "Shelley Sayer, telephone!"

"For me?" she asked, startled. She still sprang up out of old habit, even though she knew phone calls now would only come from her mom or dad or Marge, or maybe her grandma Sayer in Massachusetts.

"For you," Miss Chatham said.

Bette's voice faded behind her as she took Miss Chatham's arm and followed her into the hall.

There was a pay phone in the women's wing, but incoming calls always came through in the director's office. Shelley held on to her. Did she dare tell them about her cooking class or her walk to the corner? Her dad's blood pressure was bound to skyrocket, just picturing it—

"Hello?" she said.

"Hi, Shelley?"

For a moment her heart stopped. Then it was racing double time as she gasped, "Hi, Tom?"

"Yeah, it's me. Sorry I didn't call you sooner. I lost the phone number and had to get it from your sister."

"Oh, that's OK," she exclaimed. "I mean, it's really nice to hear from you."

There was an awkward pause. She was on the point of saying something else, anything, just to keep the conversation from shriveling away, when Tom asked, "How do you like it over there? They treat you OK?"

Across the desk Miss Chatham coughed and riffled through a drawer. "Oh, it's OK," Shelley said, floundering. "I guess I'm learning stuff."

"Yeah? Like what do they teach you? Can you read Braille yet?"

"Are you kidding? I've got my first class in that tomorrow morning. So far it's mostly just—oh, you know . . ." She slid to a stop. Tom's world revolved around school and parties and trips to the mall. How could she explain to him the thrill of successfully cutting up her own meat or finding the mailbox by herself, the relief in doing little things again that she had once taken for granted?

Tom didn't wait for an explanation. "Listen," he said, "I keep thinking about you, wondering how you're doing and everything. When do you get out of there, anyway?"

"The program lasts eight weeks. I'll be home toward the end of August."

"That's not such a long time," Tom said. "We'll be seeing each other before you know it."

"Sure," she said cautiously, trying to keep the excitement from taking over her voice. "That'd be really nice."

"I bet you get kind of lonesome," Tom said. "I'll call you again, just to see how you are. OK?"

"OK. It's always a treat to hear from the real world." He was probably only trying to be nice. She wouldn't let herself expect too much.

Miss Chatham cleared her throat. Why couldn't Shelley be allowed a little privacy to talk on the phone? She hardly knew what she wanted to say to Tom, but she might have had a better idea if the director hadn't been listening to every word she said.

"So I can tell everybody you're fine?" Tom asked. "They're not starving you or anything."

"Tell them I'm fine," she said. She wanted to tell him that she was great, now that he had called, but she couldn't say that with Miss Chatham standing over her.

"I better get off now," Tom said. "I'll call you again pretty soon. Take it easy."

"You too," she said. "Bye."

"A boy from back home?" Miss Chatham inquired, taking the receiver from Shelley's outstretched hand. "Anyone special?"

"Oh, not really," Shelley said, turning to the door. But because of that phone call, Tom had become more important than any boy had ever been before.

Chapter Four

"Wow!" Marge exclaimed. "They've got everything in here! There's even a potter's wheel! Shelley, did you make any of the things up on those shelves?"

It wasn't easy for Shelley to give the family a guided tour of the crafts room when she didn't know exactly where to point. "You see that little oblong box with a lid, kind of like a treasure chest? It should be up there someplace, drying. They don't run the kiln till Wednesday."

"Oh, Shelley! You made that yourself?" Her mother hadn't gushed like that since she brought home her first finger painting from nursery school. She shouldn't have brought them in there. But she was running out of things to show them, and she hadn't the slightest idea what they would find to talk about when it came time to sit down.

Her father grabbed Shelley's arm as they stepped down into the patio. It wouldn't do any good to tell him she went up and down

39

whole flights of stairs on her own. He hung on to her until they went back inside to the lounge, though she could have led the way herself.

Louise was in there when they arrived, her knitting needles clicking rhythmically from her traditional seat under the window. A chair scraped in one of the booths on the left, and she knew someone was listening with earphones to a cassette book.

"This is where we mostly hang out when we don't have classes," Shelley said. "Oh, I can show you where the soda machine is, if anybody wants something."

"I'll go," her dad said hastily before she could step away from them. "I saw it out there. What does everybody want?"

When he was gone, Marge spoke up suddenly, "There's this girl Jill at my school—you know what she got for her birthday?" She paused expectantly.

"A trip to Disneyland?" Shelley ventured.

"No, this is way better. You know what they bought her? A horse!"

"Really? Hey, that's neat!" Shelley settled back on the vinyl sofa. It was a relief to talk about something other than her mobility lessons and Braille classes and typing exercises. Sometimes it was hard to remember there was still a world outside the center. "Will she let you ride it once in a while?" she asked.

"I don't know," Marge said, sighing. "I don't really know her. Maybe she will if I offer to help her clean out the stall or something."

Shelley laughed, and even her Mom joined in. Marge had a herd of china horses galloping over the bookcase in her room. She felt the same way about riding as Shelley had felt about mountains and climbing.

Shelley's father returned and distributed chilled cans of cola and root beer. Careful footsteps sounded in the hall. Then Georgia, one of the older women, inquired in her West Texas drawl, "You in there, Louise?"

"Dropped a stitch," Louise said shortly. "Got to pull out four rows."

Even after a week at the center, Georgia still hadn't learned her way around. There was a soft thump as she collided with one of the easy chairs near the door. Shelley's father was on his feet in an instant. "Here, let me," he insisted. "You want a chair over there by your friend?"

Shelley had hoped her dad would relax now that she was sitting down, safe for the moment from steps and swinging doors and a hundred other perils. But, no, he was going to worry about every blind person who came into the lounge. And on a Sunday afternoon, with no formal classes, there would be a steady stream of arrivals until suppertime.

Once Georgia was settled into a cozy chat with Louise about sweater patterns, Shelley tried to steer the conversation back to Jill and her new horse. "Have you seen it yet?" she asked Marge. "What's it look like?"

"It's a gelding. Kind of on the small side, only fourteen hands." Marge had read so many horse books she talked like an expert. "He's a palomino, really gorgeous!"

Another pair of feet tapped along the hallway. "You know what Marge's going to want now for Christmas," Shelley said, hoping she might draw her dad's attention away from the doorway.

The tactic seemed to work. "Not on our budget," he exclaimed. "You know how much it costs to feed a horse for a year? Besides, they're treacherous. They'll throw you or stamp on your foot—"

Marge groaned. "I know, I know."

The footsteps stopped just inside the room. For a moment Shelley almost believed her father was relaxing a little—that time he didn't leap out of his seat.

"Dad?" It was a boy's voice, low and questioning. By now, Shelley knew the voices of most of the trainees and teachers, and she knew at once that this voice didn't belong to a regular.

"Kevin!" Howard called back. A machine clicked off, and he emerged from the listening booth. "Sorry, I didn't hear you at first. I was so engrossed in that book. You can't beat John Le Carré."

"Mom'll be over in a couple of minutes," Kevin said. "She just wanted to pick up some groceries first."

"We may as well sit here awhile, then." In a few moments Howard and Kevin had taken a couple of chairs across from the sofa.

The furniture in the lounge seemed purposely arranged to encourage people to talk to one another. It was fine during those long evenings after dinner, when there was nothing much to do but listen to one another's stories. During visiting hours, though, Miss Chatham's intimate circle of chairs had definite drawbacks. If conversation had been strained before, it was doubly difficult then, with Howard and his son sitting right across from them. But Shelley plunged ahead, before her father had a chance to look around for someone to help. "What does she call it—the horse, I mean?"

"The name on his papers is Commodore, can you believe that?" Marge said. "Jill's father kept trying to persuade her she wanted a computer instead of a horse, but it didn't work."

"The Lone Ranger and 'Hi-ho, Commodore'! The gallant steed of the eighties," Howard said, chuckling. Shelley wasn't certain whether he was speaking to Kevin or addressing the whole group.

Apparently Marge decided that he meant to join the discussion. "The horse is the eighties, but the cat's name is from the sixties," she told him. "She named her Janis, after Janis Joplin."

"Does Janis like to sing out on the back fence at night?" Kevin asked.

"She's a Siamese," Marge said. "When she meows she sounds just like a baby crying. One time their neighbors called the police because they thought a baby had been abandoned in the field behind their house."

You could count on Marge to have a story for every occasion. Maybe at last everyone was going to loosen up.

But just as Shelley began to relax, her father cleared his throat and stood up. "Well," he said, "guess we better hit the road pretty soon. Got to get up early tomorrow."

"Next time we'll get here earlier," Shelley's mom said. "We'll all go out for lunch someplace."

"Great," Shelley said, wondering fleetingly how her table manners would have progressed by then. "It's always a treat getting out of here, even if it's just to walk down to the mailbox."

Howard's wife arrived just as Shelley's family was collecting themselves to leave, and Bette appeared with her friend Maria and a boy she called Red. For a few minutes there was mass confusion around the door to the lounge. Shelley sighed with relief once the goodbyes were over. She felt as if she'd been holding her breath the entire time her family had been there. Of course, she reminded herself, she had only been at the center for a week. Maybe in seven more weeks she'd have regained enough confidence to deal with her parents no matter how much her mother fluttered over her and no matter how many catastrophes her father's imagination conjured up. Maybe.

She was making her way around a coffee

table, heading over toward Bette, when Kevin asked at her shoulder, "I've seen you somewhere before, haven't I?"

"I don't know," she answered, a little startled by his nearness. "I've been here all week."

"No, from some place else. Do you live here in Albuquerque?" Kevin asked. "Shirley, isn't that your name?"

"Santa Fe," she said. "My name's Shelley. Shelley Sayer."

"Shelley Sayer!" Kevin cried. "Sure, I remember! Climbing Thompson! A year ago spring break, wasn't it?"

"Wait a second. You're Kevin Burns! I should have figured it out—I know your father's Howard Burns."

"There was such a neat group of people on that climb," Kevin said. "I'll never forget it. You were making up ghost stories, you and that girl in braids—"

His image floated before her: he was tall and wiry, his tanned face laughing beneath a thatch of dark brown hair. Blue eyes—or had they been tinged with green? "You were the one who invented Super-Camper, with all his fancy equipment," she said. "That whole climb we kept making up stories about him, remember?"

"Hey, right! Remember the sleeping bag? Super-Camper had one with a built-in electric blanket, and he carried around a folding tent with collapsible pipes that he could hook up to the nearest stream for running water.

Kevin sat down on the sofa and patted the

empty cushion beside him. Shelley took the seat he offered, still talking eagerly. "His tent had a TV antenna and a complete sound system. And he had this nifty wall-to-wall carpet that spread out automatically when he put the tent up."

Shelley had tried for months not to think about the Thompson climb, or any climbing expedition, for that matter. But Kevin had caught her completely by surprise, making her remember. Then they were reminiscing about their struggle up the last torturous hundred feet and laughing over the exploits of Super-Camper. In their stories a helicopter always picked him up at the halfway point and he parachuted to the summit. She forgot that she was sitting in the lounge at the Center for the Blind. Once again she was off with the Climbing Club, sharing all of the excitement with someone who loved the mountains as much as she did.

"It's amazing, meeting you again like this," she told Kevin. "Are you still doing much climbing?"

"Sure," Kevin said. "There's a climb in September, on that double peak in Colorado they call the Maroon Bells. It'll get into some really challenging rock climbing. Hey—you'll be out of here by then. Why don't you sign up?"

Shelley winced. He couldn't be teasing her, he was too nice for that. Maybe he thought she was a partial like his father. Maybe he didn't understand that sometimes *blind* really meant *blind.*

"Really, why don't you?" Kevin prodded. "Maybe we can try to get that old group together again."

"I can't." Her words were just above a whisper.

She sensed Kevin turning on the sofa to look at her closely. "Why not?" he asked.

"What do you mean, why not? Do I have to spell it out for you?" Tears burned behind her eyelids. She fought to keep her voice from shaking. "It took me three days to learn my way around the center. How do you think I'd make it on a rock climb?"

Kevin was silent. She shouldn't have said so much; she shouldn't have embarrassed him. But he had demanded an answer.

"I never thought about it before," he said at last. "I wonder if a blind person'd need any special techniques besides just having people give directions. After you were roped with a partner, you could just follow along the trail. I bet you'd get the hang of it."

"I'd slow the whole team down. And if I fell or something, I'd mess up the trip for everybody else. And, anyway, what's the fun of getting to the top if you can't even look at the view?"

"Well," Kevin suggested, "you wouldn't have to worry about looking down and getting dizzy, either."

Shelley tried her best smile. "It just wouldn't be the same, that's all. If I tried, it'd just remind me all over again—about everything."

"How long have you been blind?" Shelley

winced again. As much as she hated people's awkwardness around her, she wasn't used to being talked to so directly. Kevin didn't stumble over the word, the way some people did. He just came straight out and asked.

"Since March. March fifteenth. So that's three and a half months."

"That's not very long," Kevin said. "I guess you've still got to get used to it. Maybe September's a little soon."

"You know, right before I lost my sight, I had started driver's ed at school," Shelley said. "I couldn't wait to learn, so I wouldn't have to have my mom or dad chauffeur me everywhere all the time. But then when I was in the hospital, and the doctor came in and told me there wasn't anything else they could do, I didn't even think about how I was never going to drive a car. The first thing I remember thinking was I wouldn't be able to go climbing anymore—" Her voice was shaking, out of control, but now that she had started speaking, she couldn't stop. "I thought, well, I may as well turn in my Climbing Club card. Won't need that now!" she finished bitterly.

"So did you?" Kevin wanted to know.

She didn't reply at once, fighting to master her feelings. "No," she admitted. "I've got it still. Along with all the pictures I took from all the different hikes and climbs I went on. They're at home in my bottom desk drawer."

"Hey, Kevin! Where are you?" Howard called across the room. "Come on, you haven't told me about your job!"

"OK, just a second," Kevin said. He turned back to Shelley. "Guess I've got to go," he said. "We just live two miles from here, so I'll probably get over again some night this week. Maybe I'll see you around."

"Sure. I'm not going anywhere."

"Nice talking to you," Kevin said, getting up. "So long."

"Bye," she said, getting up, too. She bent to pick up her cane and laughed softly to herself. A lot of good a cane would do her on the Maroon Bells!

Yet the seed of the idea Kevin had planted was already sending out shoots. Suppose he was right! Maybe climbing would come back to her once she started; her hands were already remembering how to fold slacks and wash dishes and so many of the other things they had done automatically before March.

But climbing mountains wasn't just a familiar series of motions done over and over the same way. It demanded everything mentally and physically; it forced the climber to make decisions every foot of the way. And the moments of pure awe—they captured the entire being, as though the climber had been transported into a dimension beyond ordinary time and space.

No. She couldn't think about those things anymore. For her the challenges of life had shrunk from mountain peaks to shoelaces and silverware. Her only excitement would come from triumphing over simple, day-today tasks, in mastering bits of life that other people took for granted.

Kevin had caught her off guard, but from now on she would be more careful. She wouldn't torment herself again with memories of climbing. She would forbid all hopeless dreams of the glory of the mountains.

Chapter Five

The first time Pat, the Braille teacher, placed a Braille page on the table in front of her, Shelley was half afraid. Her fingers tentatively explored the meaningless smear of dots, searching desperately for a pattern, a hint of meaning. The letters Pat tried to show her were nothing like print letters at all. "The Braille system is based on a rectangular cell composed of six dots, kind of like the six on a dice," Pat explained. "All of the letters are combinations of any number of those six dots. For instance, *A* is the dot in the upper left-hand corner, all by itself. The upper and middle left dots make *B*. The two across the top of the cell are *C*."

But that first morning, and for one or two mornings after that, Shelley's fingers felt numb and wooden as she probed the page. She could scarcely distinguish two dots from three, much less recognize their positions.

"It's always hard at first," Pat assured her.

"Don't worry. In a couple of weeks you'll be reading sentences."

And she was, after a fashion. At the end of her third week of classes, she read from the bulky book on her lap, as laboriously as a first grader, "Tom is a cat. Tom eats mice. Mice hate Tom."

She paused to run her fingers over the lines again. *Tom!* His name was captured within this precise arrangement of dots. Maybe she would show him what it looked like. Maybe he'd want to learn to write Braille himself, so he could send her letters she could read on her own. He'd written her twice, and she had asked Marge to read the letters to her when she came to visit. Shelley had wanted to read them over and over again, but she couldn't ask anyone at the center, or even Marge, to do that for her.

Shelley heard a faint click as Pat snapped the lid of her Braille watch shut. She'd have to get a watch like that herself. Then she wouldn't have to pester other people anymore, asking the time. Pat's watch popped open when the stem was pressed and the positions of the hands inside could be felt. The twelve was marked with two dots, and there was a single dot for each of the other numbers around the face.

Like so many things she'd discovered since she arrived at the center, the idea of a Braille watch was simple and logical. But each new gadget was a fresh revelation for her. Not only were there Braille watches, there were

Braille rulers, measuring cups with raised markings, and bathroom scales that talked!

"I guess that's enough for today," Pat said, pushing her chair back. "You're definitely coming along. Next week we'll work on the contractions."

"Already? I can hardly keep the alphabet straight." Bette had warned her that there were at least four hundred abbreviations or contractions in Braille, for groups of letters like *th* and *ou*, and for common words such as *good, about,* and *under.* Bette contended that she'd never read much besides comic books when she could see, and there was no way they were going to make her learn four hundred shortcuts.

"It's not so bad as it sounds," Pat assured Shelley. "Before you know it, the whole system will be second nature."

"It is for you, maybe," Shelley said. "But you said you learned Braille when you were a little kid."

"That made it a lot easier," Pat admitted. "But I've even had students in their sixties and seventies who managed to learn."

Pat was the only blind teacher at the center. Sometimes Shelley found herself wondering if Pat's life would be a blueprint for her own. But Pat revealed almost nothing about herself. As Shelley rose to leave, she gathered her courage and asked in a rush, "Do you have your own apartment?"

"Sure," Pat said. "All to ourselves—me and Alexandra. She's my cat, or I'm her person, that's how she looks at it." Shelley couldn't help but smile. Pat not only had her own apartment, she also had a little pet that depended on her.

"You'll do fine," Pat said. "Just give it time, everything'll fall into place." She seemed to know that Shelley worried about more than learning Braille.

Sure, time helped with a lot of things, Shelley thought as she made her way down to the dining room for supper. Cutting up food, keeping track of which blouses matched which pairs of slacks—all of those things were becoming easier every day. But there was more to life than managing the "activities of daily living" as Miss Chatham called them. Perhaps, no matter how many skills she mastered, nothing awaited her but isolation and an aching loneliness. Perhaps Pat had a cat because she had no one else.

What would happen if Shelley went back to school in September? With a pang she thought of Cindy, the girl with cerebral palsy who had been in her math class sophomore year. She had avoided Cindy whenever she could, and when they came face to face she never could think of anything to say. Cindy always seemed so glaringly strange, with those clattering metal braces on her legs and her slow, labored speech. In Cindy's presence Shelley felt uncomfortable, as though at any moment she would do precisely the wrong thing.

Now she would be the strange one. Would she ever fit back into her old crowd? Would she be invited to Melissa's slumber parties? Or would she find herself a member of that collection of misfits Lorna once christened the Odd Squad?

She swept back a stray lock of her short wavy hair with her free hand and straightened her shoulders. Why was she dragging herself down with all those grim thoughts? Tom was coming! He was driving down to Albuquerque with his folks to see an uncle, and he was stopping by the center. If a guy like Tom was still interested in her, she had nothing to worry about.

But as she sat in the dining room, picking at her meat loaf and mashed potatoes, anxiety grew within her. What would Tom think of the center, she asked herself for the hundredth time. It was one thing for him to keep in touch with her from a distance. Talking across the wires they were equals—he couldn't see her any better than she could see him. They could discuss their old friends and Tom's summer job at the hardware store. But once he saw her swinging that long, red-tipped white cane or caught a glimpse of one of her massive Braille volumes, three times the size of a regular print book, neither of them would be able to pretend any longer.

She left the table before dessert was served. Back in her room, she stood perplexed before her open closet. Around there she didn't worry too much about what clothes she put on; not even the partials could see well enough to notice whether her skirt and top were the best combination or if her blouse brought out the highlights in her red brown hair. Of course Ms. McDougal, the grooming instructor, made a big fuss the other day when she accidentally put on striped jeans with a checkered shirt. It was an embarrassing moment, but she knew everyone else in the group had slipped up at one time or another. Out in the real world, though, such a mistake would be unforgivable.

Carefully she slid the first hanger along the rod. It was a short-sleeved cotton blouse. She could picture it exactly with its light flower print; it was cool and summery. Now if she could just decide what to wear with it. Impatiently she pushed aside the blue corduroy skirt that her mom had insisted she bring, just in case the temperature dropped. Then came two more tops, a filmy white one with a tie at the throat, and something soft with a stiff collar and heart-shaped buttons at the wrists. It belonged to that limbo category of new clothes, clothes her mom had bought for her after she came home from the hospital, as though all that shopping would ease their misery like a magic potion. She remembered her old clothes as vividly as the faces of the people from back home. But the new outfits, like all of the new people there at the center, brought forth no visual memories. She recognized people by their voices, and clothes by their shape and texture. But she didn't have much faith in the pictures of them she conjured up in her imagination.

She slipped her hand inside the collar of the mystery blouse and read the tiny metal label she had sewn inside, a project in Ms. McDougal's class. There were the Braille letters *gn*. Green. The next blouse was labeled *pp*, for purple.

She wanted something casual but pretty, feminine but not frilly—the flower print blouse. She'd wear it with the jeans she had on already. She pulled the blouse from the closet and put it on.

"Shelley Sayer? You have a caller."

Shelley whirled around toward Miss Chatham's voice, still smoothing the front of her blouse with one hand. "Already?" she gasped. "He said not till after seven."

"He's waiting in the lounge," Miss Chatham said brightly. "Come on, you look fine."

"Do I really?" Miss Chatham was a sorry substitute for a mirror, but she would have to do.

"Just run a comb through your hair. There. Ready now?"

"I guess so. Ready as I'll ever be."

Traveling through the halls by herself was easy now. She walked purposefully toward the lounge, guided just below consciousness by the echoes of her footsteps against the walls and ceiling. Once or twice she reached out to touch the wall, just to double-check where she was. Her cane was folded neatly into its four short sections, and she kept it tucked out of sight in her shoulder bag.

It wasn't the old fear of crashing into furniture or being caught off guard by a flight of stairs that made her heart pound that night. Her entire being concentrated on putting forward an image of calm and normality, on holding her apprehension at bay. At the doorway to the lounge she paused, studying the scattered rustlings and voices for clues. If she knew where he was sitting, she could walk right up to him and say hi. She could melt the awkwardness with her ease and nonchalance.

But she had no idea where he might be. After a few burning moments, when he still didn't rush forward to greet her, she called faintly into the void, "Tom?"

"Oh! Shelley!" A chair scraped back, feet struck the floor, and he swept toward her in a gust of confusion. "They told me you were still eating. I'm sorry, I should have been watching for you."

"That's OK," she said quickly. "Were you waiting long?"

She felt the tension in his hand as he took her arm and led her to the sofa. "Not very," he said. "I was just looking around. All those cassettes in the plastic containers are books?"

"Over there?" She pointed toward the listening booths. "Yeah, the Library of Congress puts them out."

"It must be nice to just relax and let a tape recorder do the reading for you," Tom said, laughing a little uncertainly.

"It's relaxing, all right. Half the time it puts me to sleep."

"Oh. Maybe it would be hard to get used to."

There was an unnaturally long pause. Dessert must be over. Someone's cane rattled against the leg of a table. Howard laughed in the doorway, and she caught Kevin's voice, recounting some story about the neighbor's dog. She wanted to join their conversation, to retreat into the usual center routine. But that was crazy! She'd been longing for Tom's visit all week. She didn't want to be rescued, she wanted to make it a glorious success.

"Hey," she said, "why don't we get out of here? There's a coffee shop around the corner."

"I haven't got much time. See, my uncle's in from California because he's going to some sales convention. And we're all supposed to go to this fancy restaurant at eight o'clock." The answer came so quickly Tom might have rehearsed it.

There wasn't room to argue. It was Shelley's turn to say, "Oh." Her face grew warm again.

Bette's giggle from over by the windows punctured the deepening silence. Eddie muttered something about old Chatham wearing soundless slippers so she could snoop around to her heart's content.

Shelley had to say something. "You want a soda?" she asked. "There's a machine down the hall."

In an instant Tom was on his feet. "I'll go," he said. "I'll be back in a minute."

Shelley sank back against the cushions,

wrapped in despair. He couldn't wait to get away from her. He'd probably invented the whole story about going out to dinner so he wouldn't have to stay too long.

But to Shelley's relief, Tom really was back in only a minute, placing a Styrofoam cup in her outstretched hand. "I brought some corn chips, too," he said, sitting down beside her again. "Do you like them?" Or would you rather have potato chips instead?"

"These are fine," she said, digging into the crackling bag. "Thanks."

"This place isn't bad," Tom said after a moment. "I mean, it's not like I expected."

"What did you expect?"

"I don't really know. Dark, for one thing. I guess I had this weird idea—you've got a place full of, you know, people that can't—anyway, I guess I thought nobody'd bother turning on the lights."

"Oh, sure," Shelley said, mustering a laugh. "Why waste electricity, right?"

"And I kind of thought they'd have everything padded." Tom spoke more easily now, laughing a little himself. "Like maybe they'd have some kind of foam rubber on the walls, so nobody'd get hurt if they bumped their head."

"They'd have to put padding on all of the people," Shelley said. "The biggest collision since I've been here was between Bette and Louise the other morning."

She stopped. She didn't want to spend the sliver of time they had left talking about the center. Anything would be better—baseball, the weather, TV. But she couldn't find the right question to get the conversation moving.

And then, when she was certain that in another moment he would spring up and announce with poorly hidden joy that he really had to run, Tom half rose from the couch. But then Shelley heard the rattle of a newspaper. "Oh, hey!" he exclaimed. "Somebody left today's *Journal* on the coffee table. I bet the comics won't put you to sleep."

"The comics!" she cried. "Is 'Peanuts' in there? Or how about 'The Wizard of Id'?"

Tom flipped through the pages. "Here," he began. "Lucy's got her sign up, 'Psychiatric Consultation,' and she's talking to Charlie Brown. He says, 'I've been talking to you for three months now, and I still don't feel any better.' And Lucy says, 'Well, you don't feel any worse, do you?' Charlie Brown says, 'No, I guess not.' And Lucy says, 'That'll be twenty-five cents, please.' "

They groaned and laughed together. Tom read "Blondie" and "The Wizard of Id" and described another cartoon with no words. She would never have dreamed that comic strips could be funny without the pictures, but somehow Tom's voice brought the scenes to life.

As Tom read one strip after another, Shelley realized that his audience had grown. Soon the other conversations in the lounge had faded, and they were all laughing together, again and again, out loud. This was the Tom Travis she had always known—the class vice-president, the boy who could capture a crowd and hold its attention. She glowed with pleasure and pride that it was her visitor, her friend from outside who was entertaining them all.

He read the horoscopes and a crazy letter to Ann Landers. The regret in his voice couldn't have been for show when he sighed and said, "Well, I really better head over to that restaurant or my mother'll kill me."

She rose and walked with him to the door. "I wasn't sure what it'd be like, having you here," she confided. "Only, now, I really am glad you came."

"Me, too," he said. They stepped out into the hall, away from the jumble of voices and laughter in the lounge behind them. And suddenly, swiftly, his arms were around her. He pulled her to him, held her for a long, dizzying moment, then slowly let her go.

"Listen, I'll be talking to you," he said. "Don't worry about anything. I mean, everything's going to be OK."

"I'm not worried about a thing," she told him. And all the way down the corridor back to room 205, her feet, usually cautious and uncertain, never touched the floor.

Chapter Six

In the old days, when her mother worked late at her souvenir shop on Thursday nights, Shelley had cooked dinner for the whole family. She had thrived on the responsibility as she stirred soup in one of the big cast iron pots or thrust a pan of rolls into the oven to warm.

Then, after Shelley had returned home from the hospital, her mother claimed her work schedule had changed. The new girl at the shop could handle everything beautifully on her own, so Shelley's mother came home for dinner Thursdays.

Shelley hadn't protested. What use could she be surrounded by steak knives and sizzling pans? In the kitchen she had become obsolete.

But at the center she found herself assigned to Mrs. Pardo's home economics class every Monday, Wednesday, and Friday morning at ten. "Think of cooking as an adventure," Mrs. Pardo would urge the class in her bright, twinkly voice. "Anything a sighted person can do in the kitchen, there's a way you can learn to do it, too."

Little by little Shelley came to believe her. She learned to chop vegetables, curling her fingers safely out of the way against her palm and locating the flat of the knife blade with her knuckles. She found that she could hear the rising bubbles as a pot of water came to a boil and feel the firmness of a hamburger that was properly browned. Her lingering fear of the stove faded, and she discovered that she could even hold a burning match at just the right spot to light the gas oven by herself.

In home repair class, Tuesdays and Thursdays at two, she changed light bulbs, spliced wires, and hammered nails along with an occasional finger. She was learning to touch-type, too, every morning at eleven. If she went back to school in September— something she allowed herself to dream about now—she'd be able to turn in her assignments in print.

So Shelley gradually settled into life at the center. Her busy schedule left little time for brooding. As the weeks passed she found herself laughing more often, forgetting for longer and longer stretches of time that her life had fallen to pieces.

The high point of the week came on Friday afternoons, when all the trainees clambered into the center's minibus and drove to the pool at the nearby YMCA. Floating in the cool, refreshing water, Shelley thrilled with a sense of grace and freedom. No one pretended that swimming was a class. It was pure fun, the break they all needed at the end of a demanding week.

She would have been almost happy, if it hadn't been for mobility training.

Mr. Donaldson assured her that she had mastered the basics of cane technique, and she knew she walked far more smoothly and swiftly than she had ever dreamed she could. By the fifth week she had progressed to advanced lessons: crossing Center Street, taking city buses, finding specific stores in a shopping mall. She listened to traffic patterns to determine when the light was in her favor; she asked the bus driver to let her know when they reached the street she wanted. She recognized the supermarket by the clatter of grocery carts, and the mingled smell of soap and perfumes and medicine let her know when she came to the drugstore.

She was no longer afraid of falling into an open manhole or getting hopelessly lost on an unfamiliar street. Yet she couldn't shake the feeling that she looked like a freak, swinging her long white cane from side to side as she hurried down the sidewalk. Once, as she and Mr. Donaldson boarded a bus, she heard two women behind her talking in muted voices. "So courageous, won't let it stop her . . . so young, too . . . such a shame . . ." Another time, as they waited at a busy street corner, she heard a tense whisper: "Joey, stop staring at that blind girl!"

"There isn't much more I can teach you at

this point," Mr. Donaldson told her one day two weeks before the end of the session. "What you need to do is to start going for walks on your own. When you've got an hour between classes, walk over to the drugstore for a Coke or just take a stroll around the block."

"There's never that much free time, really," she argued. "I guess I'll have plenty of time to go for walks once I get back home."

Mr. Donaldson's long, disapproving pause was more eloquent than any lecture. She rifled her brain for some excuse he would accept, but nothing came to her. "That'll be your assignment," he announced. "Before class tomorrow afternoon, go out for a walk somewhere, anywhere, by yourself."

When supper was over, Shelley and Bette usually drifted down to the lounge. They'd often find Eddie and Marco debating whether to play rock or country-western music on the stereo, and tiles would rattle as Rob and Joanne prepared for a game of Scrabble. Georgia and Louise could almost always be found chatting in the corner.

The lounge wasn't exactly an exciting place to spend one evening after another, but it was comfortable. Someone always had a story to tell, and as they shared the events of the day, Shelley felt she belonged to a strangely assorted but generously understanding family.

There were times, though, when she grew bored with the endless talk about disasters in cooking class or what Miss Chatham and the instructors must really be like in their private lives.

And just as Bette had foreseen, the center operated on a strict code of regulations. Beds had to be made and rooms swept every morning before breakfast. Women were required to wear skirts or dresses to dinner. A ten-o'clock curfew was observed every night except Saturday. Bette grumbled and fumed and plotted rebellion. Shelley could understand the business about cleaning their rooms, it was all part of being responsible and self-reliant. But if the center wanted them to be independent, why couldn't they stay out after ten? It was as if they were only expected to be competent adults within limits. Beyond a certain point they had to be monitored and protected.

Some evenings, when Shelley sat in the lounge feeling bored by the conversations and frustrated by the regulations, the center would close around her like a cage, shutting her away from all the dazzling variety she thought she remembered in the outside world.

Maybe that was why she enjoyed her conversations with Howard's son, Kevin, so much. He had started a job at the Exxon station eight blocks away, so he dropped by almost every night when he got off work. He'd visit with his father, then sooner or later he would turn to Shelley.

Kevin hadn't brought up climbing after the first evening. But one time he startled her by asking if she could play chess. When she admitted she knew nothing about the game, he began to teach her. The chessboard was easy enough to use, it had raised squares, and the white pieces were flat on top while the black ones were rounded. Planning a strategy was the real problem.

Kevin was a patient teacher, but within a few evenings the chess lessons began turning into long talks instead. He told her about his friends, his job, and the tame fox he'd had when he was twelve. She hold him about her trip to the East the year before, about her cousin Ruth who was a ballet dancer, about some of the eccentric tourists who wandered into her mother's shop. As the days passed, she felt they were really getting to know each other, that he really saw her as a friend and not just one of the center residents to whom he should be politely friendly.

The evening that Mr. Donaldson had assigned her the walk Shelley could think about nothing but the walk as she ambled into the lounge with Bette. Eddie's choice of music had won out that time, for the room exploded with the pulsing of drums and the twang of electric guitars. Bette disappeared, probably setting out in search of him, and Shelley sank into the vinyl-covered sofa. She knew she was being ridiculous, but she couldn't put the solo walk out of her mind. She had to start going out on her own sometime, but she wasn't ready yet. No matter how many pep talks she listened to, no matter how many instructors built her confidence, she'd never be able to face the pitying whispers and the curious stares that were bound to follow her wherever she went.

A second cut on Eddie's album was fading, when the cushion shifted slightly and someone settled onto the sofa beside her. "Hi," Kevin said. "Why do you look so serious?"

"Hi!" Shelley said. "When did you get here?" She ignored his question.

"Just a minute ago," Kevin said. "It turns out my dad's not even here. He had to go somewhere with Ralph, his partner. They'll be a while, they're thrashing out some business together."

He hadn't forgotten his question. "What were you thinking about before I came in? You looked kind of sad."

"I'm supposed to start going for walks alone," she said. "You know—with my cane."

"Oh," Kevin said. "You're worried about it?" She had guessed he would respond that way.

"I shouldn't be," she said. "Only I don't know if I can make myself do it. I'll just keep thinking up reasons not to go, and the time will go by, and at four o'clock Mr. Donaldson with ask me how I did and I'll have to tell him how I didn't."

"Where are you supposed to walk to?" Kevin asked.

"Anywhere. As long as I go by myself."

"I don't start work till three tomorrow," he said. "Why don't we meet someplace? You know where the park is?"

"The one with the swings and stuff for the kids? Yeah, I think so."

"You could walk over there and meet me at two, if you haven't got a class then."

"It's Wednesday—I haven't got a class." Shelley forced a laugh. "I can't think of any reason not to, except that I dread stepping out onto the sidewalk by myself."

"I bet it won't be so awful once you do it," Kevin said. "Anyway, why worry about tomorrow before it gets here?"

If Kevin hadn't been waiting for her at the park, Shelley never would have persuaded herself to push open the front door the next afternoon. But he *was* waiting, and at two o'clock she set off down Gonzalez Street. It was the hottest time of the day, and she seemed to have the whole sidewalk to herself. She began to relax. In spite of the searing sun it was a pleasure to walk along, thinking her own uninterrupted thoughts. With a jolt, she realized that that was the first time in over four months that she had gone out alone. Perhaps her life really could get back to normal after all.

Then she scolded herself for letting her thoughts wander. She had been relieved that no one was on the street to stare, but that meant no one was there to point her in the right direction. Suppose she couldn't find the park! What if Kevin waited for hours while she wandered aimlessly up and down silent, empty streets?

A wild panic seized her, forcing her to a dead stop in the middle of the sidewalk. She'd turn around, she'd retreat to the center. Kevin wouldn't wait too long since he had to be at work. She'd explain to Kevin that she just couldn't make it.

No. She had to go. Kevin would worry if she didn't show up. She willed herself to think rationally. She knew the way to the park. Cross Center and turn right at the other side, then walk three blocks to Mendoza and turn left, and the park is half a block down. She couldn't get lost. She'd be there in ten minutes, if she just kept cool.

She reached the corner and waited, listening intently to the thundering trucks and cars. At last there was a lull, and a car started up on her left. It moved parallel to her, in the direction she wanted to go, so that she had the light.

She was about to step from the curb when a hand gripped her arm. "Step down, honey, that's a girl," came a woman's voice. "I've got you, don't worry."

"Thanks," she said mechanically as the woman propelled her across the street. She tried to feel for the opposite curb, but her rescuer was holding her right arm, so she couldn't use her cane properly. She half stumbled up onto the sidewalk and tried to slip free of the woman's grasp with another dutiful, "Thanks a lot."

"Where are you going, dear?" the woman asked. She had a heavy, middle-aged sort of voice. "I'm not in a hurry, I'll take you where you want to go."

Well, she thought ironically, she wouldn't have to walk alone after all. But something, perhaps the way the stranger had called her "dear," made her flinch. "You don't need to," she said politely. "I'm OK." She turned and started along Center Street.

"This is a very congested street," the woman said at her shoulder. "I'd better come with you." Overriding Shelley's protests, she seized her arm once more and continued, "You must live over there at the home. Isn't there someone who can watch you? You shouldn't be out alone—it's dangerous."

"That's what I'm learning, how to—" Shelley began.

But her companion swept on, "How long have you been—uh—in this condition?"

In what condition, Shelley wanted to ask. How long have I had light brown hair? How long have I been sweltering from the heat? "How long have I been blind? A couple of months."

"A pretty girl like you—it's a tragedy! I'm so sorry, dear!"

"It's not a tragedy," Shelley said fiercely. "It's—it's just something I'm learning to live with."

The woman didn't seem to hear her. "Your mother must be heartbroken," she said, jerking her to a stop at the next curb. "Was it an accident of some kind? Can't they do anything for you?"

It was more than she could endure. "I don't even know you," she said, amazed by the anger rising in her voice. "I was just minding my own business—walking along—and all of a sudden I'm supposed to answer all these personal questions. You wouldn't dream of coming up to me and prying into my life if I could see!"

"Well, I only meant to—"

"I'll be fine, thanks," Shelley broke in.

The woman dropped her arm. "Well, I won't be angry," she said. "I'd be bitter myself, if I were in your condition."

Shelley's knees were still shaking when she heard the shouts of children in front of her and the creak of swings which signaled the park. "Hey, you made it!" Kevin called. "Come on over here—there's a bench in the shade."

Dizzy with relief she staggered toward his beckoning voice. "What's the matter?" he asked, hurrying to meet her. "What happened?"

"I'll never do that again as long as I live!" she gasped. "It was awful! It was worse than I ever thought!" "Why?" Kevin said. "You got here on time, you didn't get hung up anywhere."

She took the arm he offered, and he led the way back to the bench. When they were settled, she tried to tell him the whole story. Kevin listened sympathetically as she repeated all of the woman's questions and remarks. But when she trailed off at last, he merely

73

said, "You can't let people like that stop you from doing what you want."

"That's easy for you to say," Shelley said, flaring up. "You don't understand! I feel so conspicuous; I know people stare at me. It's as if my life is public property or something. I'm not just me anymore, I'm this oddity for people to wonder about!"

Kevin had no answer to that. "Come on," he said after a moment. "Let's walk around and see if there's anything interesting going on."

She didn't have the energy to try using her cane again. She gratefully accepted Kevin's arm, and together they explored the park. They splashed their faces with cool water from the bubbling fountain and listened to a girl who strummed a guitar and sang in Spanish. Kevin showed her an abstract cement sculpture, almost as tall as she was, with lots of pits and ridges to serve as toeholds for climbing children.

"What time's it getting to be?" she asked finally. "You said you have to be at work by three."

"I do have to start thinking about leaving," he said and sighed. "You can find your way back if I walk you out to the street, can't you?"

"Not again! Not right away!" she cried. "Did you drive here? Could you maybe drop me off?"

"I could, I guess," Kevin said. "Only maybe you ought to try walking back. Kind of like getting onto a horse again after you fall off, you know?"

"It'll always be impossible. This afternoon just proves it."

"Maybe you shouldn't take people like that lady so seriously," Kevin suggested. "You give them too much power, you let them run things."

"I don't feel like talking about it," Shelley said. She heard the quaver in her voice. "Please, could you just take me back to the center, just this once?"

He was silent, weighing his decision. "If you really insist," he said slowly. "I just keep thinking you shouldn't give up so easily. You sure you want a ride?"

She was positive, but somehow his tone shamed her into shaking her head. "OK, I'll walk," she said reluctantly. Her voice was under control, but she was furious. He was practically refusing to drive her, forcing her to struggle back alone.

"I have a feeling it'll be better this time," Kevin told her when they reached Mendoza Street. "I'll probably see you tonight—you can tell me all about it." He gave her hand a reassuring squeeze, and she started back the way she had come, tapping her cane rhythmically before her along the sidewalk.

Ten minutes later she climbed the three familiar steps and pulled open the heavy front door of the center. She had found her way back with no trouble at all. She wouldn't be quite so afraid the next time she went out, and the time after that might be even easier.

That night when Kevin arrived she would tell him about her blissfully uneventful walk, and she would thank him for not giving her a ride. They would laugh together when she confessed how angry she had been at him for a minute or two then admitted that he had been right all along. She was truly lucky to have found a good, sensible friend like Kevin.

Chapter Seven

"Howard never knew he had such a devoted kid before," Bette remarked, stirring through the contents of her bureau drawer as she and Shelley packed their belongings to go home.

Shelley paused in the doorway. "What are you talking about?"

Bette laughed. "The first week Kevin came once to visit his father, right? Then he started showing up maybe twice a week. Now he's here just about every night."

"His job is so close," Shelley pointed out. "He drops over when he gets off work."

"Yeah, you're right," Bette said. "And that's why he's going out with you tonight, too. Hah! I bet Kevin's got something else in mind."

Could Bette be right, Shelley wondered as she started down the hall. It just didn't make sense. She enjoyed talking to Kevin, but there was no hint of romance in his relaxed, easygoing manner toward her. She never thought of Kevin as someone to date, as a potential boyfriend. If anyone would ever fill that role in her life again, it would be Tom. He had liked her before she became blind; he knew the real Shelley, not the temporary trainee at the Center for the Blind. If Tom were beside her, she might pick up her old life where it had broken off last March.

All week the tension within her had mounted as each passing day brought her departure a little closer. Life at the center did have a comforting routine. Although it grew monotonous at times she liked Bette and the rest of the group. They understood and accepted one another.

But the center was an island, and she couldn't stay marooned there for the rest of her life. Ready or not, she had to get back to Lorna and Melissa and the ordinary concerns of an ordinary life. And she had to be with Tom again.

She had regained some confidence in her ability to live her old life. Maybe getting back in with her old crowd wouldn't be any harder than learning to comb her hair or walk by herself. Being with Kevin had shown her that she really could feel comfortable and natural with other people. Soon her friends would forget the awkwardness they had felt in the beginning. They'd realize she was still the same Shelley Sayer they had always known.

Kevin waited for her in the lounge, hurrying forward even before she stepped through the door. "Hey, you look nice," he exclaimed. "I've never seen that skirt before.

"You in the mood for tacos or hamburgers or what?" he asked as they headed for the front door.

"Anything that's not going to spill," she said, trying to laugh. "I still feel like some kind of public menace in a restaurant."

Kevin cleared his throat to launch into a protest just as Miss Chatham overtook them. "Going out now, Shelley? That's nice. Don't forget we lock the doors at ten. You'll be in by that time, won't you?"

"Sure," she answered, more abruptly than she had planned. One thing she wouldn't miss about the center was Miss Chatham and her everlasting list of rules.

Determined to be as independent as possible, Shelley walked beside Kevin down the sidewalk, tapping her cane ahead of her as she went. His car was parked halfway down the block. "This is your big night out," he said as she slammed the door. "Where do you want to go?"

"How about the taco place?" With tacos she wouldn't have the hazard of pouring on catsup. The worst that could happen was that some of the lettuce and cheese would fall out of the shell onto her lap.

"We're off!" Kevin said, putting the car in gear.

They settled into a corner booth, and a girl with a distinctly Back East accent took their orders. "Ah, the lilting strains of the mariachis," Kevin said above the twang of a country song that whined from the jukebox. "Just imagine them serenading beneath your window, senorita."

"Ah, yes!" Shelley giggled. "And breathe in the fragrance of the bougainvillea flowers!"

"Oh, no!" Kevin exclaimed. "You forgot! I should have reminded you!"

"What?" she cried, rigid with alarm. She had forgotten to cut the tag off her new blouse, or she had put on a brown shoe and a black one—

"Flowers! Senorita, you should have worn a flower in your hair!"

"Listen," she said, laughing. "If your imagination's good enough to hear mariachis in this place, it can dream up a whole crown of flowers!"

Kevin turned serious once the food arrived. "So," he said. "You're going home tomorrow. Are you scared?"

All of the teachers at the center had been telling her for weeks that she was doing beautifully. Pat claimed she was getting so proficient in Braille that in a few more months she'd be reading just for pleasure. Even the dour Mr. Donaldson offered her high praise when she caught the bus in front of the shopping mall, got off at the right corner, crossed Center and arrived, unassisted, in time for lunch. And Miss Chatham kept repeating that she was "making a wonderful adjustment." Kevin was the first person who ever asked her how she felt about it.

"I'm terrified," she replied as something slivered from her taco and plopped onto her plate.

She braced herself for him to tell her she had nothing to be afraid of, that she had mastered all the techniques for survival, that the worst was definitely behind her. "Terrified of what, mostly?" he asked.

"Everything! I don't even know where to start." She thought a moment, digging into a mound of refried beans. "Going back to school—I don't know how I'll even keep up with the work. And being around my folks. My mom and dad really bring me down every time they come here. And then, being around all my friends. I mean, everybody'll be nice and all, but—" She hesitated, but the words got the upper hand. Uninvited, they came out in a rush. "All the kids at school who are a little weird, the ones nobody wants to be seen with, they'll all lumped together in the 'Odd Squad.' And that's where I'm probably going to land."

"The Odd Squad?" Kevin repeated. "That's great! Who's in it, anyway?"

"Liza Wartski. She's so attached to her mother she calls home every day at lunchtime. And Mary Jane Riley—she's so shy she blushes if you just say hi to her. And Abel Tovar. He's some kind of mathematical genius, but he can't communicate with regular people."

"But you communicate fine," Kevin pointed out. "You're not peculiar or anything."

"No, I'm perfectly normal—at the center.

But when I go back to school, I'll be the only blind kid there. I've hardly heard from any of my old friends since I came to Albuquerque, and sometimes I get this awful feeling I've lost them all!"

"If they're your friends, though," Kevin said, "why should you lose them?"

"I don't know. I try to tell myself I'm just worrying about nothing, but—" She forced back her fear. "Maybe it won't be so bad. Tom will make it easier."

"Is Tom that tall, blond guy who came to see you a couple of weeks ago?" Kevin asked.

"That's him. He's been great through this whole thing. All the other guys I knew kind of disappeared, but Tom—he's still here."

Kevin was silent. If she could only search his face for a skeptical lift of an eyebrow, a pitying frown puckering his forehead! Kevin was a boy. He'd know if Tom still saw her as the girl he took to the Christmas dance, pretty Shelley Sayer with the silky, brown hair and deep blue eyes or whether Tom just felt sorry for her and wanted to be kind.

But why did she need reassurance? She couldn't forget the feel of Tom's arms so tight and strong around her. "I don't think I appreciated him enough before," she went on thoughtfully. "We went out a couple of times last winter. He seemed nice enough, but I wasn't serious about him. Only now"—she drew a long, quavering breath—"now it's like I don't know how I'd dare to go back if he wasn't there."

It was almost too much to say. Embarrassed, she turned her attention to the last of her taco.

Kevin seemed willing enough to change the subject. "I was thinking," he said. "We've still got plenty of time. You want to go to a movie?"

"I guess so—sure." After all, the TV was always on in the lounge, and she had discovered she could figure out most of what was happening on the screen by listening carefully. She sometimes lost the story during car chase scenes, but then the good guys always finished first in a car chase, anyway.

The show they selected didn't start until seven fifty-five. It was a real tearjerker, but at least there weren't any car chases. To Shelley's relief no one in the nearby seats complained when Kevin leaned over to whisper a few crucial details of the action.

Shelley didn't think about the time again until Kevin mentioned it when they were nearly back at the center. "You think Miss Chatham will make you stand on the sidewalk all night?" he asked. "It's ten after ten already."

"Oh, no!" For a second she felt that awful sinking sensation in her stomach, the feeling she had gotten when she was a little kid and the teacher sent her to stand outside the door for talking in class. But she was almost sixteen now; it was silly to be afraid of Miss Chatham and her scoldings. "She'll have to let me in if I knock, but then I'll have to listen to her lecture about how the rules are designed for our own protection, and just because I'm leaving tomorrow doesn't mean I can disregard them, etcetera, etcetera." She paused and added slyly, "Bette came in at midnight the other night. She found a door to the basement that wasn't locked."

When they stepped out of the car, they walked to the front door. But when Shelley tried the knob, it wouldn't turn. She lifted the heavy brass ring that served as a door knocker, then set it gently back into place.

"Well, what do you think?" Kevin asked when she turned to him. "You up for an adventure? Want to go look for Bette's secret door?"

"Anything's better than listening to Miss Chatham," she told him. "Come on."

Arm in arm they descended the steps again and entered the alley between the center and the house next door. Leafy bushes brushed Shelley's face as they skirted the building. Once Kevin tripped over a loose brick, nearly making Shelley lose her balance as well, and it was so funny that they could barely suppress their giggles. "There's an open stretch coming up," Kevin whispered. "The moon's really bright tonight. Anybody could see us. We better run for it."

He grabbed her hand, and together they pounded across a gravel drive to crouch at last, panting and laughing, in the shelter of the next clump of shrubbery.

"You sure Bette got in a door?" Kevin asked in a low voice. "All I see so far are windows."

"She said it was a door into the laundry room. I think she stayed out late on purpose, just to see if she could outwit this place."

"If she could do it, we can do it," Kevin promised. They got to their feet again and cautiously made their way along the unyielding wall. By then they were on the far side of the building and couldn't hear even the sound of distant traffic. Crickets rasped in the grass, and the faint roar of a jet reached them, muffled and far away.

"All right!" Kevin's whisper rang with excitement. "There's a door over here, just like you said."

"Is it locked?" Shelley ran her hand across the dusty wooden panels and found the handle, gritty with rust.

"To open or not to open," Kevin intoned, and they both started giggling again.

Shelley pulled on the handle, and nothing happened. "They locked it!" she said. "Bette's got a charmed life."

"Try pushing," Kevin advised. She lifted the handle, put her weight against the door, and it crashed inward so suddenly she almost fell. With a giddy surge she caught the sweet scent of detergent.

"Want me to come in with you for a minute?" Kevin asked.

"Better not. Chatham'd really throw a fit if she caught me sneaking you in after visiting hours. Then we'd *both* have to listen to the lecture.

"Yeah," Kevin said. "Only it feels kind of

weird, saying good night out here with the weeds and the broken cinder blocks and all."

"It'd be worse saying good night in the house director's office," Shelley reminded him.

"Wait a minute," he said. He stepped away from her but returned almost before she had time to wonder where he had gone. "Here. Smell."

She caught a fresh, sweet fragrance. "What is it?" she asked as Kevin placed a cluster of tiny, feathery flowers in her outstretched hand.

"I don't know what they're called," he said. "They're on a vine that's growing all over the wall back here. Let me have them a second."

She handed them back, and he slipped the stem gently into her hair above her right ear. "There," he said softly. "A flower for your hair, senorita."

Something in his tone, so soft, with hardly a hint of his usual laughter, made her suddenly uneasy. Could Bette have been right after all? Did Kevin expect something more than friendship from her? Something she couldn't give him, since the real Shelley Sayer was the Shelley Sayer who lived in Santa Fe, not at the Center for the Blind.

"I better go in," she told him, suddenly confused. "No point stretching my luck."

"Well, good night then. Let's keep in touch, OK?" It was the sort of friendly farewell she would have expected. And the quick, parting squeeze he gave her hand before she stepped through the door was nothing special. The flowers simply were part of the game they had played over dinner.

"Goodbye," she whispered, leaning out into the night air for one last moment. "You made life a lot more fun around here. Thanks for everything."

She pulled the door shut behind her and stood alone in the eerie quiet, trying to get her bearings. The place wasn't the same without the busy slosh and hum of the machines. For an instant she convinced herself that she wasn't in the laundry room after all, but in some uncharted section of the basement where she would wander lost and exhausted until morning. Who knew what might lie hidden in the rooms where none of them had ever ventured?

She held out her cane, half afraid of what she might discover—and heard a glorious clang as it struck metal. Sure enough, there was the row of washers and dryers. She knew precisely where she was; she had really known all along. In another minute she was racing up the back stairs to room 205, home free. Bette would have been proud of her, finally stretching the rules a little when they didn't quite fit.

Her hand went to the cluster of flowers above her ear. She anchored the stem a little more firmly. She knew what Bette would think if she told her that part of the story. She'd laugh and say, "Well, what did I tell you?"

But Bette thought every relationship between a boy and a girl had to come down to romance in the end, and that simply wasn't true. Kevin had been a friend to her just when she needed one. They had shared a lot over the past few weeks, but they really and truly were friends. Only friends.

Chapter Eight

Shelley leaned back on her canvas chair and breathed in the fragrance of the pine tree overhead. It was so lovely to be sitting on the patio after Sunday lunch, just as she had so many times on soft, lazy afternoons in other summers.

"Really, Jim, it would be worth joining the food co-op," Shelley's mother said. "We'd get a five percent discount just by signing up."

Ice clinked as Shelley's father refilled his glass. "I'm all for discounts," he said. "If they'd just let it be that simple! Why do they insist you have to go to a 'new members' meeting to learn about their philosophy? What do I need philosophy for to buy a bag of carrots?"

"I went in there the other day," Marge said. "There was this lady chasing after these two wild kids, yelling, 'Tarragon! Tofu! Get over here!' "

"Tofu!" Shelley exclaimed. "How could you name a kid Tofu? I can't even stand the stuff."

Her mother's voice broke through the fresh

burst of laughter. "Hey," she said. "Is that the phone?"

In the sudden silence a shrill ring carried unmistakably through the open windows. "I'll get it," Shelley said, scrambling to her feet. Her heart leaped with hope as it always did when the phone rang, now that she was home again.

But her mother was up, too, her feet already hurrying toward the back door. Slowly Shelley sank onto her chair again. If it was Tom, maybe it was best to let someone else answer, so he wouldn't guess she was waiting for his call every hour of the day. But then, if her mother answered, Tom might think she was too helpless to run for the phone herself.

"Marge, it's for you," her mother said. The screen door banged behind her, and she crossed toward their chairs again, slowly this time. "It's Mrs. Martinson. She wants you to baby-sit tomorrow night."

Shelley jolted forward, her hands clutching the arms of the chair. Mrs. Martinson had made a mistake, she'd gotten their names mixed up somehow.

"Me?" Marge repeated. "She never asked me before."

"She asked for you, very distinctly," the girls' mother said. "Go on, she's waiting!"

Marge was never one to hurry, but then she moved more slowly than ever. No one spoke as her bare feet plodded steadily toward the house. At last Shelley heard the murmur of her voice from the kitchen, but as hard as she strained, she couldn't pick out any of the words.

"I'm the one who always baby-sat for the Martinsons!" she finally burst out. "I've been taking care of Amanda for two years! How can they go and ask Marge, as if—as if I'm not here anymore!"

She hadn't meant to speak. She had meant to shut the hurt and the anger inside and hope that after a while they'd be buried by more important things. But she couldn't keep it to herself. It was more than she could bear.

"Oh, I'm sure she didn't mean to hurt your feelings," her mother said soothingly. "But you have to be realistic. You've got to look at it from Mrs. Martinson's point of view as a mother."

In the lengthening silence Shelley reflected that her mother was certainly back to normal again. The doubt and hesitation that had bent every statement into a question a few months before were gone. Now it was "Be realistic," "Think of Mrs. Martinson's point of view." Her statements were firm, unshakable.

"If you need the money," her dad put in, "I can increase your allowance. Maybe it's time, anyway, now that you're sixteen—"

"I don't care about the money."

She stood up abruptly, forgetting the empty glass that she had placed beside the leg of her chair. The shattered pieces tinkled on the flagstones. "Oh, no!" she cried, dropping to her hands and knees.

"Watch out! You'll cut yourself! I'll get a

dustpan!" Her mother fluttered to her side, nudging her out of danger. "Come on in the house with me. Want an arm?"

"I'm okay," Shelley protested, but her mother was right beside her, tugging at her arm. With a sigh, Shelley limply followed her inside.

In the kitchen she made one last try. "Let me sweep up the glass, at least. I'm the one who broke it."

"I'll take care of it," her mother said brusquely. "It's nothing."

"I've been back a week, and you don't let me do anything," Shelley insisted. "I've never even been out on the street by myself. What was the use of my going to the center if—"

"I know." Her mother touched her shoulder. "I'm your mother, I just can't help worrying, I suppose. You'll feel better once you go back to school. You'll be so busy you'll complain about not having any spare time."

"I'll be busy, all right," Shelley muttered. "It'll take me six hours to do my homework every night."

"Well," her mother suggested, "why don't you go practice your Braille or work on your typing a little? You've got that home teacher coming to see you Tuesday."

Shelley couldn't answer. Her hip grazed the corner of the stove as she rushed away, and the coffeepot rattled its reproach to her back. She had been fooling herself into thinking that life was back to normal. Those easy, laughing moments out on the patio had only been an illusion. She had forgotten all the times her father's restraining hand grabbed her wrist just as she started down the steps, the dozen excuses her mother found whenever she offered to help with the dishes or the vacuuming.

Her big Braille workbook waited on her desk between its two blank covers. But she sank down on the edge of the bed, her hands empty on her lap. Even before she left the center she had known her homecoming would be difficult. Yet somehow she had hoped her parents would be as excited as she was by the things she had learned to do. Instead, they did everything they could to be courteous, but it was almost as if she hadn't been in the program.

And if her own parents were afraid around her, what could she expect from the kids at school? For the hundredth time she thought of how her friends had treated her since her return. She had phoned Melissa and Lorna right away, inviting them both over. Melissa had dropped by the other night, and they chatted randomly while the TV blared in the background. Lorna said she'd be over, but she hadn't called back. But all of that was less important, Shelley reminded herself, fanning a spark of hope, since Tom called just an hour after she stepped into the house. And he had promised he'd come to see her.

Bare feet padded down the hall and paused at the half-open door. "Shel?" Marge called softly.

"Yeah?" It was more of a challenge than a greeting.

The hinges squeaked as Marge pushed the door wider. "I'm not going to baby-sit tomorrow," she said, plunging right to the point. "She asked me, but I said no."

"How come?" Shelley asked.

Marge hesitated, not venturing beyond the doorway. "It's your job," she said. "I mean, she should give you a chance. Amanda's used to you, and you probably know their house as well as you know ours. And if the place were burning down, you could call the fire department as well as I could."

A hard knot of pain in Shelley's chest loosened. "Maybe," she said. "I thought so, until Mom started in about being realistic."

"Realistically," Marge said, "I don't think I could stand ten minutes with Amanda. She'd be worse than Tarragon and Tofu rolled into one."

"She is kind of a spoiled brat," Shelley agreed. "In a way I won't miss her."

Marge crossed the tiled floor to the braided rug by the bed. "I was just thinking, I'm going out for kind of a walk." Her voice dropped to a whisper. "You want to come?"

"What's 'kind of a walk'?"

"Just kind of a little hike. I don't know what you'd call it. It's a ways, out to a place I go sometimes."

On the TV in the living room fans roared with excitement as an announcer cried, "It's a hit!" Shelley's mother clattered around the kitchen, cleaning up after lunch. "Sure," Shelley said. "Anything'd be better than hanging around here all afternoon."

Neither of them had to say that their parents must not know where they were going. At the door to the living room Marge said breezily, "Shelley and I are walking over to Jill's to see Commodore."

"That's lovely," their mother said. "Have a good time." There it was again, that unnatural politeness that was becoming a habit now. *That's lovely.* It was the sort of thing her mom would say to a customer in her souvenir shop who had just tried on a Mexican rebozo.

The girls giggled together once the screen door had closed behind them. Marge seized Shelley's hand, and they broke into a run down the drive to the road. Shelley felt suddenly lighter, eager for whatever was to come. Still, a doleful voice pointed out, life had gotten pretty dreary when the high point of her week was sneaking out on an adventure with her little sister. Back in the old days she wouldn't have wasted fifteen minutes with Marge; Marge wouldn't have expected her to, either.

But now, as the road grew steeper and the city traffic gradually faded behind them, the exhilarating fragrance of piñon pine wafted by on the crisp breeze. A croaking swooped low over their heads. Shelley was glad she had agreed to go for a walk, even if she was a little out of breath. "How far is 'a ways'?" she asked after a while. "I'm really out of shape. This hill's getting to me already."

"A ways is—oh, you know. We'll get there pretty soon."

She knew just where they were. They'd walked a mile along Canyon Road to the edge of the town, then turned onto Camino de las Estrellas. After another quarter mile they left the road and mounted a narrow, rocky path she had hiked dozens of times before, toughening up for one of her big Climbing Club expeditions. She pictured the matchbox cars that she knew were whizzing back and forth below them and the soaring mountains above them with their peaks shrouded in purple haze. She could nearly predict each twist and turn as they wound higher and higher.

Well before they reached it, she sensed the great round-topped boulder that interrupted their path, the relic of some avalanche, which had thundered down the mountainside centuries before. As they drew nearer and nearer, their steps echoed back against its hulking presence. For the last few yards, where the path was suddenly level, Shelley let go of Marge's arm and stepped toward the rock, pulled to it by a strange magnetism she couldn't have explained.

"We better rest here for a second," Marge said. "This is where we get off the path and go overland."

Shelley leaned against the stone, running her hands over its jagged surface. It was half again as tall as she was and as long as a medium-size car. As it rested there, massive and inert, it was almost impossible to imagine that it had once crashed and bounded down the crags, heedlessly crushing trees and bushes and any wild creatures that couldn't scatter fast enough. Shelley spread her arms wide, reaching as far as she could from one end of the boulder to the other. Pressed against it, she knew, they looked as frail and insubstantial as the little doll she had had once with arms and legs made of toothpicks.

"Ready?" Marge asked, interrupting her thoughts. "This part might be a little rougher."

Shelley took Marge's arm. In three steps they left the traveled, civilized path behind them and entered a wilderness of clawing underbrush and tumbled rocks. Now and then Marge tossed out a hint of what was coming: "Big stone here, go around to your left," she said. "Here's an old rotten log, we've got to go over it," she cautioned over her shoulder. Most of the time, though, Shelley scrambled along beside her, sensing when Marge turned or stepped up or down, trusting her feet to find the surest way. The afternoon sun caressed her left cheek and told her that they faced north, but within a few minutes she had no clear notion of where they were. It didn't really matter. She just reveled in the splendor of rocks and wild bushes and high clear air unspoiled by human interference. After so many months shut indoors, she was in the mountains again.

"Now we've got to climb down," Marge's

voice quivered with eagerness. "Wait till you see this place, Shel, you won't believe it."

Shelley was startled, but not displeased, by the offhand way Marge used the word "see." Her mom and dad kept correcting themselves: "You see what I mean—I mean, you *understand*?" Each time they stumbled over their words it was a reminder—as though she needed one—that she wasn't quite like other people anymore.

The first step down put an end to her wandering thoughts. "Better turn around and go backwards, like down a ladder," Marge suggested. "That's what I usually do."

Even turning around was tricky. Shelley's feet scrabbled at a narrow ledge of rock while her hands clutched for a steady hold. But at last she was descending, her searching toes finding one uneven stone step after another. Water bubbled somewhere below, and she sensed walls growing narrower around them.

"What is this, a canyon?" she asked, panting.

"You never knew this was here, I bet." Marge's voice floated up to her, gleeful and a little proud. "I found it last summer."

"Last summer?" Shelley began. She hunted for a fresh hold, and a stone tore away from beneath her hand. She fought to steady herself, but the ledge beneath her left foot was crumbling, too. With a cry of fright and shame she lost her balance and toppled, clawing and skidding amid a shower of dust and pebbles.

In the next instant she jarred to a stop. She was crouched on what seemed to be a wide flat rock, and though her knee was bruised and she had scraped her right elbow and shoulder, she knew she wasn't badly hurt. But for a few moments she couldn't speak and didn't try to move.

"Shelley?" Marge's voice was taut with concern.

"I'm OK," she said at last. "I guess."

"I fell once here myself," Marge said, trying to console her. "It could happen to anybody."

Especially to anybody who's blind, Shelley thought grimly. She forced herself to her feet and shakily continued the slow descent.

With each step the gurgle of water drew nearer. Then Marge's feet thudded on solid earth, and she called, "You're at the last step. Sit down and slide the rest of the way, it's about five feet."

She still hadn't recovered from the fall, and Marge's words filled her with panic. She couldn't give up her last solid hold to let herself into the unknown. But she couldn't perch there forever, either, clinging to the final step. "Come on," Marge cried, and with a grating of pebbles Shelley slid down and down to the smooth canyon floor.

"Isn't that neat?" Marge chattered. "Look, there's this clear little stream that cuts straight through the middle." She took Shelley's hand and led her across a patch of tall grass. Shelley knelt down and plunged her hand into the icy water. Her fingertips barely touched slippery stones at the bottom.

"And over here," Marge went on, "is the couch."

Obediently Shelley followed her around a tangle of mesquite to a low shelf of rock recesses in the canyon wall. Thick moss covered it, soft and fluffy as a woolen blanket.

"Sit down," Marge said. "Make yourself at home. Zelda the maid will be in with the tea trays."

Giggling, Shelley settled herself on the couch and leaned back against the rocks. "This *is* neat," she said, rubbing her sore shoulder. "You found it a year ago? How come you never mentioned it before?"

"It's nice being the only person who knows about something," Marge said softly. "When you're out here, you can sing, dance, do anything you feel like."

"Didn't you ever bring Jill or anybody?"

Marge threw a pebble into the stream. "Jill's got a big mouth. She'd blab it to everybody at school. I wanted to keep it a secret."

"So why did you change your mind now?" Shelley pursued. "Why did you decide to show me?"

"You can't keep a secret forever," Marge said philosophically. "What fun is that?"

Something in Marge's logic eluded Shelley, but Marge often didn't follow the laws of reason. "Thanks," she said a little awkwardly. "I'm glad you let me in on this."

"There's a waterfall about half a mile farther up," Marge said. "And I know where there's a cave, too. I found some burnt matches in there once, though, so someone else's been in there."

For the first time Shelley felt a surge of respect for her odd, wandering younger sister. "Why don't you join the Climbing Club?" she asked. "You're probably a lot more experienced than most of the beginners they've got."

Marge threw another stone. It broke the surface of the water with a ringing splash, clear as a note of music. "I don't think I'd like to go with a big gang of people all the time," she said. "It'd make everything so complicated."

The girls sat in silence, listening to the endless chatter of the stream over its bed of stones. Not even the cry of a bird broke the stillness. Perhaps the earth had sounded like this in the very beginning, Shelley thought, before the Anasazi people left their cave drawings, even before the dinosaurs thundered. She wondered how much could be seen from where they sat—probably the circling rocks walls, widening as they rose higher to let in the light from a ragged patch of sky. She opened her mouth to ask Marge to describe everything she saw, but she didn't want to disturb the silence with questions. She really didn't need words to paint a picture of the canyon for her. The sheer wall behind her, the bubbling stream, the brittle grass under her feet, and the vast silence, shimmering with mystery, filled her imagination as vividly as if she had seen the canyon herself.

Then, in a flood of anguish, she knew she would never again have the freedom to explore these mountains alone. Sure, she could scramble over rough terrain with Marge beside her, keeping her on the right course. But even then she stumbled and fell. It wasn't fair. She had been the real climber, the daring one. Now her little sister could head off alone anytime she chose to discover secret canyons where she could dance and sing as much as she pleased, while Shelley Sayer sat home, struggling to read from her Braille workbook.

Perhaps Marge sensed the change in her mood. "We better head back," she said. "What if Mom calls Jill's house? She'll have a fit when we're not there."

"Yeah," Shelley said. "She and Dad'd die if they knew I was out here." Marge didn't deserve to be hit by the chill that had crept into her voice. None of this was her fault.

"Maybe we can come out here again," Marge said.

"Sure," Shelley said, trying to sound enthusiastic. "They watch me like a hawk, I need to get away any chance I can."

The mountains still beckoned Shelley with all of their old magic. They still awoke in her the awe which had made her challenge them over and over again. But she knew that she was no longer equal to their challenge. On a real climb she'd be in the way now, groping and stumbling and afraid to let go and drop when the time came. She'd slow down the whole expedition, maybe even endanger the others. A "kind of walk" like this only served to remind her of everything she had lost. As the girls trampled over the path back out to the road, the mountain mocked Shelley with echoes of her footsteps. Never again would she let herself be reminded of the most beautiful thing she had lost. Never again.

Chapter Nine

Tom called twice the first week Shelley was home, but he didn't make any plans to visit until the following Monday. Then at the last minute he called to say his car had broken down, and he couldn't make it into town. She knew he lived about five miles out in an exotic solar-heated home his folks had built, and obviously without a car he couldn't go anywhere. Since he had to work Tuesday and Wednesday nights, he had promised to come on Thursday.

Then Thursday afternoon his dog got into a dispute with a skunk, and Tom called apologetically to explain he'd be busy giving Freeway a bath in tomato juice. He was leaving with his family the next morning to spend a week down in Carlsbad. "I'll give you a call when we get back," he said, but didn't even suggest another date for a visit. This mound of evidence withered even the memory of that swift embrace in the hall outside the lounge.

At least she had a couple of letters from

Bette and Kevin to keep her company. One afternoon Marge brought in the mail and handed Shelley a long, thick envelope. "From Burns, in Albuquerque," she explained. "Somebody from the center?"

"Not exactly." Shelley's fingers were suddenly clumsy as they tore the unusual envelope open. She was about to hand the letter back so Marge could read it to her when she realized why it was so thick. Kevin had written to her in Braille!

Some of the dots had been flattened at the creases in the pages, and Kevin occasionally confused *F*s with *D*s and *H*s with *J*s. Those letters were very similar, and she'd made the same mistakes herself plenty of times. She worked until suppertime over the letter, laughing to herself at the way some of the words turned out, before it all finally made sense. It was thrilling to read her very own mail in private again after so long.

Not that Kevin had anything terribly personal to share. He had written just the sort of comfortable, friendly letter she might have expected.

Dear Sjelley,

I'm sitting here witj Faf's Braille writer machine and *Braille Workbook Number One*, and this is my tjird start because I make so many mistakes. I guess I'll just have to leave them and hope you can digure out what I'm saying, otherwise I won't finish till Tjanksgiving.

I keep remembering the things we talked about that night wjen we went for tacos. How are you getting along? What is it like for you being at home? Jave you seen many od your drienfs from school? What about Tom? I bet by now you've got everything under control. I know you'll hang in there, whatever happens.

By the way, did you get in all right that night? It was a crazy way to say goodbye, wasn't it? But it was fun sneaking around in the bushes. It reminfef me of a movie I saw once about a buncj of kids at a ritzy boarfing school, playing wilf pranks. I hopw you didn't have a run-in with that housemother.

Writing this is starting to be fun. I don't tjink people write letters mucj now-afays, because telephones are so handy. Back in the old days letter writing was kind of an art. Maybe someday we'll both be damous and our biographers will publish "The Collected Corresponfence of Sayer and Burns."

Probably not, though. Probably this isn't even readable.

Write back or call me sometime, and tell me what's happening in your life. I think about you a lot. Maybe one of these days we'll climb another mountain together.

Running out of paper. Keep in touch.
Bye,
Kevin

Her first impulse was to rush to the phone and dial Kevin's number. His easy, laughing voice on the other end would sweep her back to the security of the center.

But Kevin had such confidence in her; he was so certain she was making the best of everything. What could she tell him if she called him that night? That her mom and dad treated her like a valuable cut glass vase? That she scared Lorna half to death? Maybe they could play a guessing game together about Tom's next excuse for staying away. She imagined Kevin's voice, predicting, "He'll hear this rumor there's going to be a big flood, so he's got to stay home and build an ark—"

Shelley straightened up and pushed Kevin's letter back into its envelope. She wouldn't call him right away. If she gave herself a little more time, maybe she'd have something positive to report. Kevin had faith in her; she couldn't tell him she was failing. She'd justify that faith in her somehow.

For months Shelley had avoided crowds, still timid about the curious stares of strangers who pressed around her whenever she went out in public. But on Labor Day Marge persuaded her to walk the four blocks to the plaza to attend a free outdoor concert. The plaza, Santa Fe's central square, was the hub of activity in the town. Artists peddled their paintings, and Indian women sold their jewelry of silver and turquoise. The square was flanked by hotels, restaurants, and shops, so it usually was swarming with camera-brandishing tourists. But the plaza belonged to the locals as well. It was a meeting place for friends, a place to wander if you had nothing to do, a spot for events like the Labor Day concert. Clapping her hands and losing herself in the music, picking up random scraps of conversation, Shelley knew with certainty that she was a member of this gathering, sharing with all of the people around her the pure joy of the band's soft ballads and lively rock tunes.

Even the thought of school, looming only two more days in the future, no longer seemed so threatening. Maybe she could become just another face in the crowded hallway, the way she'd been just a voice at the concert. Yawning through a class on world history or cheering at a pep rally, she would be one of the gang again, as she had always been before. After a while Melissa and Lorna and the rest would absorb the fact that she was blind, and her life would be back on course again.

She was stepping out of the shower that evening, her tangled wet hair clinging to her shoulders, when her mom banged on the bathroom door. "You about through? Somebody's here to see you."

"Who?" she demanded, unable to keep her heart from pounding a little.

"Tom Travis."

Her heart leaped up, and the towel she held slithered to the floor and twined damply around her ankles. "Now?" she exclaimed. "He's here, *now*? He never even said he was coming over!"

"Should I tell him you're too busy?"

"No!" Shelley cried in panic. "Ask him to wait—just ten minutes. Ten minutes, that's all."

She lost at least one minute hunting for the new purple blouse she thought she had left folded on her pillow. One of her sandals had developed a mind of its own and gone into hiding under the bed. And there was nothing much she could do about her hair but smooth it out with a comb. Tom would just have to see it wet.

In the first instant she knew she shouldn't have worried about anything. "You look cool," Tom said, his voice full of smiles. "Cool and—nice."

The glow Shelley had felt earlier hadn't worn off. The whole day had been magic. "Thanks," she said. She felt she was blushing a little. "Why didn't you tell me you were coming? I mean, I'm glad you're here, only—"

"It didn't seem like our plans ever worked out," Tom said. "I was afraid if I promised you again, something else would come up. I didn't want you to be disappointed another time."

Against her better judgment she had come right out and told him she was glad to see him. But she wasn't about to admit that she'd ever been disappointed. "Sit down, why don't you?" she suggested. And when they were settled together on the sofa she asked, "How's Freeway?"

"My mother still won't let him in the house," Tom said. "He slinks around with his tail between his legs like he lost his last friend in the world."

"How was Carlsbad?" she asked, running too quickly through her repertoire of questions. "Did it get boring after a whole week?"

"Carlsbad was OK, I guess. Hanging around with my family that long was a drag, though. Especially my brother." In an exaggerated falsetto he mimicked, "Mom, why *can't* I get a hot dog now? Dad, I wanna go in there and play the video games!"

Shelley laughed sympathetically. "What is he, five, six?"

"Four and a half. My mom and dad kept going off places and leaving me to baby-sit. I guess he's OK, as little kids go. But he can sure cut down on your freedom of movement, if you know what I mean."

Shelley's mother interrupted their conversation with a pitcher of iced tea and a plateful of chocolate chip cookies on a papier-mâché Mexican tray. After they each had munched a handful of cookies and swallowed a glass of tea, Tom asked, "What have you been doing since you got home? You keeping busy?"

If he had asked her the day before she hardly

would have known how to answer him. Even an offhand, "Oh, more or less," would have hinted at the vacuum of the past two weeks. But now she said, "I just got home from the concert in the square. The band was great. They're from Los Alamos."

"I saw a poster about them. How do they sound?"

"They remind me of some old sixties groups a little," Shelley said. "They did some really neat songs—fun stuff and some tunes about the arms race, too."

The center had been the wrong place to have seen him, Shelley realized. But there, sitting in an ordinary living room, they were two normal people, inching their way toward each other better.

She didn't know how much time had passed when Tom finally rose to go. "Listen," he said, taking her gently by the arm as she began to walk him to the front door, "I've got to drive this way to school. You want me to pick you up Wednesday morning?"

"Oh, you don't need to. Mom's giving me a ride the first day because I've got to lug so much stuff—"

"I can help you carry whatever you've got," Tom said. "How about if I come by around eight o'clock?"

"Eight o'clock," she repeated. "That'd be great!" She stood at the door, listening until she heard his car turn at the corner, but even after he was gone, she couldn't stop smiling.

*   *   *

"Hey, this isn't an Arctic expedition, you're just going to school!" Tom exclaimed as he helped Shelley load her gear into his car. "What *is* all this, anyway?"

"Just all the junk I need for my classes," she said lightly, although she was a little embarrassed by it all. There was the portable typewriter for typing out tests and written classwork. The cassette machine and the Braille-writer—a machine about the size of a portable typewriter, whose six keys represented the six Braille dots—were for taking notes. The big cardboard cartons with their heavy straps contained the textbooks she had in Braille—ten volumes of Spanish and fifteen volumes of English grammar. A stack of little plastic boxes contained an assortment of books on cassettes—biology, English lit., and health ed. She had learned that her social studies book wasn't available on tape and might not be ready for two or three months.

She had thought of leaving most of the books at home and only taking the first volumes to school in the beginning. But her home teacher, who would be visiting her once a week for the first few months, pointed out that teachers have a way of skipping around in textbooks. Besides, if she had her taped books handy, she could work on assignments during study hall, listening with earphones.

Tom crammed in the last box and slammed the hatchback shut. "Where are you going to keep it all? It won't exactly fit in your locker."

He waited beside her, holding the door open as she climbed in on the passenger's side. "My mom talked to Mr. Higgins, the new principal. I can use a shelf in the library." She hesitated before she added, "I'm supposed to take study hall in there, too, instead of going to room one-eleven." She still didn't know why she could no longer go to regular study hall with everyone else. But the library was better than Mr. Higgins's first suggestion—that she spend study periods in the nurse's office.

She didn't mention that one to Tom. And as they rolled off down Canyon Road she didn't tell him that she was now excused from taking phys ed, that her eleventh-grade math requirement had been dropped, and—worst of all—that Mr. Higgins wanted someone from the Citizens Club to escort her from class to class. She had enjoyed a few crumbs of normality when she and Tom chatted over iced tea the other day. But it wasn't easy to feel like a normal, everyday person now, encumbered with this load of special equipment.

"The parking lot's half full already," Tom remarked, easing into an empty spot. "I thought we were going to be early."

Shelley clambered down to the pavement and waited, not sure which way to turn. Around her, other car doors slammed, and anonymous voices collided in a barrage of first-day greetings and news: "Hey, I'm in homeroom two-oh-nine . . ." "She broke up with him? You sure? . . ." "Never saw you all summer! Where on earth . . ."

"We'll need to make two trips," Tom said. She would have liked to tell him to leave everything where it was—she'd manage just fine without any of it, but she knew it was impractical. She stepped to the rear of the car and reached in to help him unload.

"I've got it, don't worry," Tom said. "You wait here. I'll take these boxes in and come back for you."

An alarm bell jangled somewhere inside her head. She didn't need any more special exemptions. "No, I can carry some of this junk. Whose is it, anyway?"

"Well, OK," Tom said a little doubtfully. "Here, take your typewriter. Ready?"

With one quick exploring hand Shelley discovered that he was staggering beneath a wavering tower of boxes—probably just her entire grammar book. She plodded uselessly at his side, the portable typewriter dangling from one hand while she held Tom's arm with the other. For all the help she was giving him, she might as well have waited in the parking lot.

Suddenly Lorna's voice broke from the nameless babble. "Tom! Shelley!" she cried, pounding toward them. "Wow! I'm running into everybody before I even get through the door."

"Hi!" Shelley exclaimed. "Who else have you seen so far? Is Melissa around? How've you been, anyway?"

"So busy it's ridiculous," Lorna said in a rush. "I was away for a while, and then I was waitressing, and—you know—the time just goes. I called you a couple of times, and there wasn't any answer. But I kept meaning to go see you—"

"That's OK, I figured you had a lot to do," Shelley said, but the words sounded too bright and cheerful to convince anyone.

Somebody else joined them, stepping quietly up on Shelley's right. Even when he spoke she didn't know who the newcomer was. "Hey, Travis! What've you got there? Is there film in those boxes or what?"

"Braille books. They're Shelley's," Tom said as if it weren't obvious enough.

"Man! They must weigh a ton!" Was it Bill Harrington—big blond Bill who sat behind her in geometry last year and used to draw monsters on the cover of his notebook? No, it sounded more like Jimmy Rodriquez, the one who played guitar and wanted to be a disc jockey.

"Shelley! Hey, good to see you!" After the thousands of hours they'd spent talking on the phone, she would have recognized Melissa's voice anywhere. Her hug was as warm as ever, and her laugh hadn't changed at all.

"Are you driving to school these days?" Shelley asked her. "You've got a car now?'"

"My brother dropped me off," Melissa said. "He's working at . . ." She trailed off, her attention suddenly pulled away. "Hey, Marianne! Where'd you get that get-up? What do you think this is, Hawaii?"

What did Marianne have on, Shelley wondered. She was crazy enough that it might have been a grass skirt. "What kind of get-up?" she asked, but in the confusion no one seemed to hear her. Bill-Jimmy gave a shrill wolf whistle, and Marianne cried, "What's the matter? Even my mother thought it was OK to wear this to school."

"This is unbelievable, Shel," Tom said. "She has on this Hawaiian T-shirt and she's wearing a lei."

Shelley laughed in appreciation. No one else had thought to explain to her what they were all talking about. Only Tom made sure that she wasn't left out.

Though she stood beside Tom right at the heart of the growing crowd, she might as well have been hovering on the fringes. Even when the talk shifted away from Marianne's outfit, it swept around and over her as though she weren't there. Lorna chattered to Melissa about her date with Doug Danvers the night before, and Marianne explained to a girl with a loud whinnying laugh that she would never, *never*, work as a mother's helper again! The boy next to her, whom she still couldn't identify, leaned across her to ask Tom whether his Datsun had decent pick-up on the highway.

In the old days boys wouldn't have leaned across her as though she were invisible. This boy would have been talking to her, or maybe showing off a little, trying to make her notice him. And she would have had a story as interesting as Lorna's about her latest conquest. How could she persuade everyone that the typewriter and the tower of boxes and the cane, which she still kept folded out of sight, were only tools, that beyond all the strange equipment she was really the same as she always had been?

Somehow she had to wedge her way into the conversation, or it would swirl away from her and leave her behind forever.

"How did you and Doug get together, anyway?" she asked Lorna. "You hardly knew him back in the spring."

"Oh, I knew him some," Lorna said. "I kind of had my eye on him." She paused as if the word *eye* had made her feel suddenly self-conscious. Shelley searched wildly for another question. But she sensed Lorna turning, moving away from her, before she could speak again. She and Marianne dropped their voices, and she had no idea what was going on until Marianne's friend uttered another whinny and cried, "Oh, let's! Right after school! Where can we go?"

In the old days she would have been in on the plans from the beginning, never questioning for an instant whether she was welcome. Now she stood motionless as a cold finger of doubt slid down her back. Through the sudden pounding in her temples she heard their rising excitement. They'd have so much to talk about, Lorna said—who turned up in which classes, what the new teachers were like. Maybe they should go to McDonald's, Marianne suggested, but someone else said no, there was a new taco place on San Francisco Street.

Shelley opened her mouth to say anywhere would be fine, anywhere they could sit and catch up on all of the news. But her throat was parched, and no words would come out. Maybe no one cared what she thought.

Then Tom's hand folded over hers. "We'll go to Domino's," he announced. "It's definitely going to be the spot this year."

There was a chorus of approval, and Shelley marveled at Tom's way of bringing a crowd together, pulling the perfect decision out of chaos.

"What do you think, Shelley?" he asked. "Is Domino's OK with you?"

Miraculously she found her voice again. "Sure. I hear Domino's is going to be *the* place this year," she said, her voice light and breezy.

"That's great," said Lorna, and for the first time she spoke to Shelley without a hint of strain in her voice. "It'll be like old times again, the bunch of us hanging out after school the way we always used to."

And it would be like old times, Shelley told herself with a secret glow of happiness. As long as she was with Tom, the others would see that she was still one of them.

A couple of people volunteered to help carry in the rest of her gear from the car. Shelley picked up her typewriter again and walked beside Tom as the crowd grew denser around them. Every few yards, it seemed, they stopped to greet someone new. But at last they pushed through the heavy glass doors into the foyer. Her summer of doubt was over. The Center for the Blind was a hazy memory. Just as she had hoped, the real Shelley Sayer was back to stay.

Chapter Ten

Once Shelley's books and other equipment were stowed in the library, Tom walked her to her homeroom. Julie Mendez from the Citizens Club rushed up to introduce herself before they reached the door.

"Mr. Higgins asked me to help you get to class and stuff," she explained. "He gave me a copy of your schedule. First period you've got English, that's in room two-oh-one—"

"Listen, thanks," Shelley said, floundering, her face aflame. "I really don't think I'll need you to take me anywhere. I mean, I remember how the school's laid out. I'll be able to find my way."

"Anyhow," Tom added, "I can go with you in the beginning, till you get the hang of it."

Julie sounded relieved herself as she turned away. "Well, OK," she said. "If you need anything, get in touch with us."

When Shelley and Tom compared schedules, it turned out that they had English and social studies together every day, and they both were assigned to sixth period lunch. But all day long, even when they weren't in the same classes, he somehow managed to be there almost as soon as the bell rang, gallantly prepared to escort her to her next destination.

"I've got to start doing this on my own," she said when Tom met her at the end of the day. "I mean, I can't expect you to do this forever."

"I don't know why not," Tom said, squeezing her arm. "Now I've got the perfect excuse to hold your hand."

"Oh, come off it," she said, giggling, but she didn't argue anymore.

The halls vibrated with the double excitement of the first day of school and the end of the day. Unknown voices shouted, locker doors swung open, people pushed and shoved in their hurry. Even with Tom beside her, someone shouldered Shelley roughly out of the way. Moments later a boy pounded past, racing toward someone far down the hall, and knocked a volume of her Spanish book out of her hand.

Shelley froze, suddenly swept by a tide of despair. Those teeming corridors were nothing like the glorious, clear halls of the Center for the Blind. How had she ever imagined that she could walk from one room to the next on her own?

"What a creep!" Tom exclaimed, stooping. "I should get his license number, report him for speeding." He straightened up and handed her the book, dusty but intact. "See? I can be useful now and then, can't I?"

"Thank you," she said, and she wasn't only thanking him for gathering up *Cuentos y Conversaciones*. She couldn't turn everything she felt into words. She only hoped he understood how much she needed his easy laugh, his caring, his assurance that nothing was really any trouble at all. She would have been lost without him.

By the time she finished her Spanish homework that night, Shelley was exhausted. Reading Braille was still a tedious chore even in English, and struggling through a paragraph in Spanish took a half hour. And Spanish wasn't her only homework. It was nearly ten o'clock when she had sorted through the first container of cassettes and found tape one of the biology book. The reader was a woman who kept her voice bland and impersonal as she plowed through the introduction to unit one. At first Shelley paced up and down her room, forcing herself to concentrate on the endless stream of hollow words. At last she settled into the rocking chair by the window and rode gently back and forth, back and forth, seeking a hidden rhythm in the rise and fall of one sentence after another.

She jolted awake when the telephone rang. "Shelley, it's for you!" Marge yelled from the kitchen. "It's a guy!"

Tom! As she hurried into the hall, trying to wake up, the cassette player droned on behind her about proteins, the building blocks of life.

"Shelley!" Kevin exclaimed when she lifted the receiver. "Could you read my letter all right?"

"It was great," she said with a stab of conscience. "You don't know what a treat it was to get a letter I could read to myself."

"Really? I'll send you another one. When I didn't hear from you, I started wondering—"

"I meant to call you!" she said, plunging in before he could finish. "Every day I'd think about it. Only—only—it's hard to explain. I wanted to wait till I had something really neat to tell you about."

"What for? What makes you think everything's got to be perfect before you can talk to me?"

"I don't know," she said, laughing a little. What *was* it about Kevin? He didn't do anything to make her feel guilty, but she still wanted to be able to tell him she was doing great things, not freezing in fright in the school hallway.

"We started school today," Kevin went on. "I got the worst English teacher in the whole place—they call her Annie the Axe."

"We went back today, too," Shelley said.

"What's it really like being back there?" Kevin asked, turning serious.

"It's—it's—" She stopped, searching for words. "Today wasn't exactly a picnic, but I'm starting to think it's going to be OK. Tom walked around with me to all my classes and helped me through the cafeteria line, and after school a whole gang of us went to this place called Domino's for hamburgers."

"Sounds great."

"It was," she said fervently. "I was afraid the other kids would kind of back off from me, you know? But when I'm with Tom, it's like they see I'm still me."

Kevin was silent for a moment. "So you don't think you're headed for the Odd Squad after all?" he asked.

"I thought I might be this morning," she admitted. "There I was with all those Braille books and things. I know everybody was staring like crazy. But after school, sitting there at Domino's, I felt like things were back to normal." She hesitated. "You know, the weirdest thing happened. We got up to leave and we were all the way out to Tom's car before I realized all of a sudden that the whole time I was in there I hadn't thought once about being blind."

"Well, why should you?" Kevin asked. "I mean, if you were just sitting there eating and talking—"

"Listen, when it first happened it was on my mind every second! And this afternoon we must have been there almost an hour, and I was having so much fun, it didn't cross my mind one single time."

"That *is* great," Kevin exclaimed.

"And after today school should get easier," Shelley hurried on. "Maybe even Lorna will start to relax after a while. And Tom says he can drive me most days because he goes my way anyhow. . . ." She trailed off uncertainly into Kevin's silence. Maybe it was talking about Tom that made her uncomfortable with Kevin. For an instant her mind flashed back to the center, and she heard Bette's teasing voice: "I bet he's got something else in mind. . . ." But what she had with Tom was nothing like her friendship with Kevin. Kevin had been a real friend when she was lonesome and frightened and in despair. Tom had been interested in her before her illness, and he still was—her blindness had just changed the situation a little bit.

"My dad and I have been working on our Braille together," Kevin was saying when Shelley tuned back into the conversation. "I've finally got all the letters down, and I'm even starting to work on some of those contractions. OK if I send you another letter?"

"I owe you one first," Shelley reminded him. "I'll type it—I need to work on my typing even more than my Braille right now."

"We've got to save all our letters," Kevin said. "Keep them on file, for the 'Collected Correspondence.' "

Tom walked Shelley from class to class for the rest of the week. By the next Monday morning, however, Shelley had resolved it was time to brave the halls alone. She loved Tom's company, and she dreaded battling her way through the crowds by herself. But whenever she thought of the center and remembered her solo walks through the busy streets of Albuquerque, she knew that she was taking the cowardly way out.

Tom was skeptical when she brought up the subject on the way to school. "Why make things any harder than they have to be?" he wanted to know. "It's no hassle for me to walk with you."

It *had* to be a hassle sometimes, she knew. To meet her at the end of fourth period he had to run all the way from the annex building. With a pang she remembered what he had said about his little brother: "He's not bad as kids go, but he sure can cut down on your freedom of movement."

"You're starting to sound like my mother whenever I offer to take out the garbage," she said, forcing a laugh. "Last night she took the pail right out of my hand."

Tom didn't reply, and for a moment she thought he was concentrating on the traffic. When he spoke at last, his voice was tight. "OK, go ahead. I don't know why you want to put yourself through it, but it's up to you."

"You don't mind, do you?" she asked, startled.

"Why should I mind?" Tom said, and he sounded more like himself again. "It's just that I hate to think of you fighting your way through that mob scene." He took one hand from the steering wheel and reached over to take her hand. "I worry about you, you know."

He wasn't just being nice, he really liked her! It had to be true. If she didn't matter to him, he certainly wouldn't worry about her getting around the school building.

"I'll survive," she assured him. "I've got to start sometime."

"You've got guts, that's for sure," Tom said, and she glowed with pleasure when he squeezed her hand.

So he didn't meet her at her homeroom to walk with her up to their English class. When the bell rang, Shelley gathered her books and typewriter case with one hand, unfolded her cane, and headed for the swirl of footsteps and voices which was the open door.

"Isn't Tom coming to get you? You want me to take you somewhere?" a girl called behind her.

"No thanks," she said. She got a firmer hold on the typewriter, drew a deep breath, and stepped out into the hall. People pressed all around her, all talking at once, all sure where they were going. She must have looked grotesque, she thought, dragging a typewriter and her enormous books and flailing her white cane around. Walking along with Tom, sharing some little event or other from the last class, she never felt clumsy and conspicuous. Girls walked with their boyfriends all the time, arm in arm, hand in hand. When she was with Tom she kept her cane folded up, safely out of sight.

There was no way to keep it out of sight now. It tangled among hurrying feet, and she heard a boy mutter, "She shouldn't use that thing in here. She's gonna hurt somebody with it."

If she kept close to the wall on her right maybe she wouldn't bump into so many people, she thought. But when she got near enough to the wall to feel safe, a locker door swung out at her, grazing the side of her head. A little farther down, she nearly stumbled over a girl who, for some unaccountable reason, sat on the floor with books strewn all around her. Cautiously Shelley maneuvered past her, aghast when the corner of a book skidded from under her foot.

At first, when she noticed that the crowd was thinning a little, she felt a surge of relief. But as the flow of people dwindled to a trickle, panic rose in her chest. She hadn't even found the stairway yet! By now Tom was probably picturing her lost and frantic, or sprawled somewhere on the floor, too discouraged to get to her feet again.

The bell rang just as she found the stairwell at the far end of the hall. The echoing silence told her that she was alone, and she ran all the way up to the second floor. The hallway was laid out exactly like the one below, and the door to 217 was the first one beyond the left turn. If she hadn't felt time slipping away from her with every step, she might have known a wonderful sense of freedom as she walked along. No lockers swung open to hit her now, and there was no one to stare at her as she slid her hand lightly along the wall counting doorways.

But she was late. And when she reached room 217 at last, the teacher already had closed the door.

Slowly her fingers traced the embossed metal numbers nailed to the door just at eye level. Two-one-seven. She had found it all right, without any help from anyone. But what difference did that make now? On the far side of the door the teacher's voice rose shrilly above the scrape of a chair, "We're working in the Warriner book today. Turn to page forty-seven."

The longer she delayed, the worse it was going to be. Perhaps she could still walk in without creating too much of a scene. After all, other people were late to class all the time. The year before she wouldn't have given it a second thought.

As softly as she could, she opened the door and stepped inside. Still the teacher went on explaining infinitive phrases. Shelley's seat was the second one in the fourth row, which meant she had to walk right across the front of the room. She couldn't possibly be more visible! She shifted her books and typewriter around, and with her left hand counted the desks, one for each row. As easy as one, two, three—

"Mr. Sandoval, move your books out of the aisle!" The teacher's voice rose to shrill indignation. She scampered to Shelley's side and clutched at her arm as someone scrambled to clear a path for her.

"It's OK, nobody had to move anything," she said, but her voice rang too loudly through the stunned silence.

The teacher didn't seem to hear her. "I'm going to have to change my seating chart," she said, half to herself. "Margot, switch seats with Shelley. It'll be easier for her if she sits by the door."

Her hand clamped over Shelley's wrist, she led her back the way she had come, to the first seat in the first row.

Mortified, Shelley sank onto the chair. She folded her cane and shoved it into her shoulder bag. If she could only hide *herself* as easily, crawl into the far corner under the cabinets where no one could stare at her again.

Tom rushed to her side as soon as the bell rang. "What happened?" he demanded. "You couldn't find the right room?"

"Nothing much happened," she tried to assure him.

"Let me walk you down to your next class," Tom said. "Come on, it's hardly even out of my way."

She felt a sudden flash of irritation. "No! No thanks," she said sharply. In the next instant she was stricken with remorse. If she wasn't careful, she'd drive him away from her. But somehow she had to let him know that this was important. "I've got to start being more independent. I made up my mind I'm going to go everywhere by myself today. Even the cafeteria. I'm going through the whole line on my own."

Even as she spoke, she knew it was a crazy promise. Fighting through the corridors was bad enough. How could she hope to find a table in the cafeteria, carrying a trayful of dishes? But she couldn't back down. She couldn't let Tom think he had to baby-sit all day long, that he was stuck with her the way he had been stuck taking care of his little brother.

She didn't have much trouble finding her next class, but she was late for biology. She had to stand and listen as Mr. Richards declared, in front of the whole class, that she was the most courageous person he had ever met. Even then, she thought the morning was going pretty well until she wandered into the wrong room as she hunted for her health ed class. She was trying to figure out why someone else was sitting in her seat when a strange teacher asked, "Are you lost? This is mechanical drawing." Someone called Don was assigned to take her to room 133. During their excruciating walk to the next corridor, neither of them uttered a word.

Maybe Bette or Howard could even have dredged some humor out of that one. Shelley was beyond laughter. And she knew that she simply couldn't face the cafeteria alone. She wouldn't give up on it forever. She'd try it Tuesday, Wednesday at the very latest. But nothing on earth could make her attempt the tumult of the lunch line and the cafeteria that day.

Tom would help her, she thought as she left health ed. He'd probably be waiting for her inside the doorway. But she couldn't run to him for help now, not after that speech about doing things on her own. She couldn't admit defeat.

She remembered that the girls' washroom was at the very end of the hall, the door on the left. She slipped into one of the booths and leaned against the wall, grateful for the chance to be utterly alone while she gathered her thoughts. The longer she stood there, the more she wanted to stay right where she was. She wasn't hungry, anyway. And she had a Hershey bar in her purse. She'd eat it quietly by herself and rest. Just rest.

Tom would worry when she didn't show up at lunch. He might hunt for her everywhere.

She'd think of something to tell him. She had a headache—maybe it was big enough to justify staying away from the cafeteria. He wouldn't have to worry for long, she'd see him in social studies the next period. By then she would think of some way to explain.

The bell rang for the beginning of sixth period. She could have dashed down to the cafeteria; the halls would be empty and clear. But her legs were too weak and rubbery to carry her that far. She sank onto the edge of the toilet seat and slowly drew the bar of chocolate from her purse. It was a little squashed, but she didn't care. On climbing expeditions a Hershey bar was always good for a jolt of energy. If she had ever needed one in her life, she needed it then!

The door of the washroom opened and closed with a *swish* and footsteps clacked across the floor. She held her breath. Suppose it was a teacher on hall patrol, prowling around to make sure no one was cutting class!

Even if it was just another girl, she didn't want to be discovered. She needed some peace, some time all to herself—

"Shelley? You in here?"

Melissa's voice was low, but it shattered the silence. With a pang, Shelley remembered the portable typewriter and the pile of Braille books she'd left on a chair across from the sinks. It would be impossible not to answer.

"Yeah, I'm here." Shakily she stood up and stepped out into the room, crumpling the empty candy wrapper.

"Didn't you hear the bell?" Melissa exclaimed, her voice flooded with relief. "We all thought—everybody was afraid—and Tom sent me in here to look for you."

"What do you mean, everybody was afraid?" She swayed and caught the edge of a sink for support. She hadn't escaped at all; she had just created another problem.

"Well, Tom was waiting for you by the cafeteria," Melissa said. "And when you didn't come he started getting worried. And Lorna and I were there with him, so we asked Mr. Brinkley if we could come up and find you, and—"

"Can't I ever just be late anymore?" Shelley groaned. "I felt like sitting in here for a while, I just wanted to get away from it all, and you guys turn the place inside out!"

Melissa didn't reply. She rummaged noisily in her pocketbook, and a comb crackled through her hair.

"I mean, it's nice of everybody to be concerned about me," Shelley went on. "But I really can take care of myself. Even if I get lost for a couple of minutes, I'll figure things out eventually."

"I wouldn't have your guts," Melissa said at last. "I don't know how you do it. It must be awful, living in the dark all the time."

"It doesn't seem dark, exactly," Shelley tried to explain. "It's more like—like there's this misty veil in front of my eyes. Sometimes I picture things around me so clearly I almost think I'm seeing through it."

"But how do you walk around by yourself? I close my eyes and try to think how I'd get across the room, and it freaks me out."

"It freaked me out, too, for months," Shelley said. "But you get used to it bit by bit. It stops being this big challenge. You just walk across the room because you want to get out the door."

"You make it sound easy," Melissa said. "I bet I wouldn't be as brave as you are, though."

"People that rush into burning buildings to rescue babies are brave," Shelley stated. "They could stay outside and save themselves. They're making a choice. But I haven't got any choice to make. I'm just living my life."

"I guess so." Melissa didn't quite sound convinced. But her voice brightened as she went on, "I'll tell you one thing—Tom Travis sure has a thing for you."

Shelley stood up straight. "You think so? Really?"

Melissa sighed. "You know how most guys

are—they tell you they can't live without you, and then you fall on your face and they don't even notice. Every time I see you and Tom I get jealous. He's always thinking of you, what you might need, what you'd like best."

"Yeah," Shelley said tentatively. "Only I keep worrying maybe he just feels sorry for me."

"He wouldn't spend all that time with you if he just felt sorry for you," Melissa said. "I used to think he was just concerned with his image. Running for vice-president last year and all. But now you can tell there's a lot more to him than that."

"He's pretty special," Shelley said, and there was a little catch in her voice. "If it weren't for him I'd probably be going nuts now. He makes a big difference."

"Speaking of Tom," Melissa said, snapping her purse shut, "we'd better go out there and tell him you're alive and well."

Shelley went to the chair where she had left her things. "Come on," she said. "I think I'm ready." She felt light and graceful as they stepped back into the hall. Even the heavy books and the typewriter no longer weighed her down. And she knew that her sudden burst of energy hadn't come from the chocolate bar. Tom really was the one who made the difference.

Chapter Eleven

After his stint as sophomore class vice-president, it seemed only natural that Tom should run for president of the junior class when elections came up in October. "I like all the planning and scheming and figuring things out," he confided to Shelley, driving her home one afternoon. "When I got to be vice-president last year I never thought it'd be so much fun, working on all these crazy school projects. But it's neat, really, running things behind the scenes."

"You mean, because you get to make decisions, and have some control?" Shelley asked. This was a side of Tom she still didn't fully understand.

"Something like that." He laughed and added in a theatrical, sinister voice, "I have acquired a thirst for power!"

Shelley laughed, too. And when he asked her, with a burst of excitement, "Hey, you want to be my campaign manager?" there was only one answer on earth she could give. "I'd love to!" she exclaimed.

"Let's have a conference on it right now," Tom said, squeezing her hand.

Class elections were to be held on October 15, which gave them three weeks to prepare. Shelley spent hours on the phone organizing her committee—Melissa, Lorna, Lorna's boyfriend, Jim, and Marianne—to make posters. She wrote a short article for the *Echo*, the school paper, about Tom's political platform—which was a bit of a challenge, since the class wasn't exactly divided by burning issues. Both Tom and his opponent—Len Moreno, who'd been their sophomore class president—promised to raise money toward the best yearbook and the best prom in history. But Tom emphasized that all of the fund-raising projects would be fun, like a big junior class dance and maybe a talent show. Len made the mistake of suggesting yet another sale of magazine subscriptions, which, Tom gloated, would lose him two hundred votes right up front.

Shelley liked organizing and dashing for important phone calls. But best of all, the campaign brought her and Tom closer together. He still read her their social studies assignments, since her taped version of the book hadn't yet arrived, and helped her when she had too much to carry. But she was helping him now, and she was thrilled with the knowledge that he needed her.

Despite Melissa's reassurance, she couldn't completely erase her nagging doubts about how Tom felt about her, however. He drove her back and forth to school, and sometimes after school they joined the others at Domino's.

But they didn't really go out on dates—not the way they had sophomore year. Perhaps Tom didn't think she would enjoy movies anymore. Maybe they didn't go to the Booster Club dance at the end of September because he was afraid she'd be nervous about moving around the crowd. She wished she could ask him, but she hated to say anything, especially since he was so thoughtful about helping her in every way.

Most of all, she wished he were more romantic. He often held her hand as they walked together, but she was still waiting for a kiss or even another embrace like the one that had captured her back at the center. "Some guys just aren't very demonstrative," Melissa insisted. So Shelley reminded herself that Tom showed his feelings for her in a dozen other ways.

Then she scolded herself for expecting even more from Tom. As it was, their whole relationship was lopsided. Tom gave her his time and energy and attention, and she had so little to offer him in return!

At least the campaign for class president gave her an opportunity to be needed, to be useful, to prove her real value.

If only she didn't have to make a speech!

The campaign manager's speech was a time-honored school tradition, and asking to be excused from it would only attract unwanted attention. The campaign assembly was always held the day before the election itself. Each of the candidates and each of the campaign mangers spoke in turn before the entire class.

Writing the speech wasn't the bad part. Shelley worked on it for nearly a week, copying and recopying the Braille pages until she had every word precisely where it belonged. When she finally read it to Tom, she almost knew it by heart.

"I like it," he said when she was finished. "I like it a lot."

Shelley glowed. "You don't think I have to spell it out more—the part about your being on the track team and all?"

"It's perfect the way it is. Anyhow, the way you deliver it, that's the best part."

"Come on," she protested. "I'll probably drop the pages and get them all mixed up, and start reading the end before the beginning."

"Just keep smiling like you're smiling now," Tom advised, squeezing her hand. "And they'll love it, even if you read it in Chinese."

Tuesday night Shelley shut herself into her room and stood at her desk, trying to imagine the stage, the lectern, the packed auditorium as she read the speech aloud again and again. It wasn't long—Tom timed it at two and a half minutes—and even if she did get her notes mixed up she could almost recite it from memory. But how could she stand before hundreds of people? It was bad enough being stared at in the halls, catching whispered phrases whenever she answered a question in class: "She's incredible!" "I'd kill myself if . . ."

There were still times when she longed to become invisible, to crawl into a dusty corner and hide forever. And now she was going to deliberately put herself on display. If she had been asked to give a speech for a class assignment she might have found some excuse to stay home the next day. But she was making this speech for Tom. She couldn't skip school that day if she had awakened with double pneumonia.

The morning of the speech, Tom arrived a half hour earlier than usual. When they reached the school, Shelley listened as he rehearsed his speech one final time. His speech was just about right—modest but not falsely so, confident without slipping into arrogance, enlivened here and there with a light joke. Tom had a good speaking voice: strong and clear and rich with feeling. She remembered how he had drawn an audience when he read her the comic strips that long-ago evening at the center. Len Moreno didn't stand a chance.

The school band sounded tinnier than usual at the assembly. It blared out the school song as the junior class filed into the auditorium. Mr. Higgins stamped about, getting the candidates into their proper places onstage. He rushed up to Shelley and brought his face very close to hers when he spoke, as if she might be deaf as well as blind. "Who's going to

140

lead you up to the microphone? Or would it be better if someone brought it over to you?"

"I'll walk to it by myself," she said, trying to lean away a little without being rude. "Tom showed me where it is."

Mr. Higgins patted her arm. "Wonderful! Wonderful!" he said, then hurried on.

The band wheezed its final gasp. Shelley barely heard Mr. Higgins's introductory remarks as she leafed through her bundle of note cards. "Relax," Tom whispered beside her. "You'll be great."

"Hey, it's your show," she whispered back. "You're the one they'll really listen to."

If only she could get her speech over with! But first there were the nominees for class secretary, then for class treasurer and class historian, and finally class vice-president. After a while all of the speeches blended together: "the most capable . . . responsible . . . reliable . . . get the job done . . ."

Time was running out. Bobbi Fernandez, Len Moreno's campaign manager, stepped to the microphone. More words, more applause. Len's speech was simple and straightforward. He said that he hoped the people who had elected him the last year were happy with the job he had done and would see fit to elect him again. A burst of clapping and cheers from the back rows proclaimed that he had a loyal following, and for just a moment Shelley wondered if Tom might have some real opposition after all.

The applause died away, and Mr. Higgins

read from his list, "Now, campaign manager for Tom Travis—Shelley Sayer."

The roar of her applause nearly threw her off her feet. In the first instant she thought that perhaps she had risen too soon, maybe they were still clapping for Len somehow. But they couldn't have been. Mr. Higgins had announced her name—and Tom's. Maybe that was it. They were clapping for Tom already.

The applause still clattered about her as she started for the microphone. Through the haze of noise and confusion, she tried to remember the course Tom had helped her to map out. Two steps forward, then four steps to the left. One—two—three . . . Her legs wobbled. Suppose she were veering to the right, toward the edge of the stage? What if she tumbled headfirst into the footlights? She hesitated, extended a searching hand, caressed the empty air before her.

No one was clapping now. Here and there she thought she heard a murmur of sympathy. What was the matter with her? She was exactly where she belonged, and the microphone would be there if she took one more step!

Suddenly, before she could lift her foot again, Tom was at her side. "Right here," he whispered, guiding her hand to the lectern. "Stand back a little—there!"

There was no time to thank him or to think about what had happened. Tom disappeared again as swiftly as he had come, and she stood at the microphone with her handful of notes. Heart racing, she drew a shaking breath and began, "You probably know who Tom Travis is, even if you've never met him personally. He's been involved in activities ever since freshman year—"

The microphone distorted her voice, flung it back loud and hollow. She floated in a strange half dream, listening to herself recite the lines engraved in her memory. And as though she were standing beside herself, she heard her words for the first time and knew that she was delivering a speech like all the others before it. "Achievements on the track team . . . business manager for the Drama Club . . . experience as class vice-president . . ."

She was almost done now. She wouldn't panic on the way back to her seat, either; she'd walk calmly and quietly, and no one would have to rescue her.

She flipped to the final note card. "So if you want ours to be the best-run class this school has ever known," she concluded, "vote for Tom Travis, the man with the track record."

The ovation crashed like summer thunder as she turned away from the microphone. Cheers and applause rocked the room. She never knew how she waded through the din, but at last she sat on her folding metal chair once more, while the clapping still pounded on and on. It was all wrong, she wanted to cry above the noise. She had only given an ordinary, everyday speech, as dull as all the others; she was only ordinary, everyday Shelley Sayer. She didn't deserve all of that adulation—she had never wanted it, she didn't want it then! But even if her voice could carry above the tumult, would anyone understand what she was really trying to say?

Shelley knew that Tom had won long before Mr. Higgins declared the outcome of the junior class elections over the public address system the next afternoon. She ought to have been ecstatic when his name was announced, she thought. Tom was the junior class president, and she had earned a share of his triumph. He was liked and admired by the majority of the eleventh grade, and now all the world knew that she was the girl who stood by his side.

Yet she couldn't disperse the cloud of uneasiness that had hovered around her since the assembly. She couldn't quite bring her thoughts into focus, but she sensed that something was wrong.

Tom was waiting for her in the hall when she emerged from Spanish class. The instant she heard his voice, she pushed aside all her doubts. "Congratulations!" she cried. "You won! You really did it!"

"*We* did it," he corrected her, laughing. "I couldn't have done it without you!" Then he swept her into his arms and kissed her swiftly on the lips.

"I mean it," he said, stepping back a little, but still holding both her hands. "Moreno had a lot more support than I thought, but you made the difference."

Her lips tingled with his kiss. Her legs were weak with happiness. It was just what she had been waiting for.

"I've got an officers' meeting at three-fifteen," Tom was saying. "Would you mind taking the bus home, this once?"

"Of course not. You'll have a million things to talk about. Call me tonight and tell me how it goes."

Actually, she didn't mind the thought of taking the bus at all. She loved riding back and forth to school with Tom, but as she hurried up to her locker after the final bell her happiness was touched with a sense of excitement as if she were about to embark on an adventure.

She was rummaging for her locker key in the bottom of her purse—she had replaced the standard-issue combination lock with a padlock from the hardware store that she could manage herself—when someone called from the end of the hall. "Hey, Shelley! I thought I'd catch you here!"

"Melissa!" she exclaimed. "What's up?"

"Nothing special," Melissa said. "My brother's picking me up. You want a ride? I figured Tom'd be busy this afternoon, and I hardly ever get to see you anymore, since you spend so much time with him."

All the way down the hall Melissa chattered about her high hopes for her latest diet. If you ate half a grapefruit before each meal, she claimed, you could eat as much as you wanted! As they approached the stairs, Shelley unfolded her cane and tapped it ahead of her until she found the top step. Melissa went right on talking unperturbed.

"Hey," Melissa said at the foot of the stairs, "I forgot to congratulate you. You and Tom, that is."

"Oh, thanks. Tom will be really good, he's got a lot of ideas."

"They say it was a real landslide," Melissa said. "I can't stand the way some of Len Moreno's friends are going on about this, can you? Talk about sore losers!"

"What do you mean?" Shelley asked. The little cloud of doubt floated back. "*How* are they going on?"

"Oh, you know." Melissa hesitated. "Saying it wasn't fair, you making the campaign speech. Stupid stuff like that."

"That it wasn't fair?" Shelley repeated. "Why—?"

"It's nothing, really," Melissa said hastily. "You know how people get. They'll look for an ulterior motive in anything."

The cane shook in Shelley's hand. She stopped and faced Melissa, demanding an answer she didn't really want to hear. "I guess I don't know what you're talking about," she said carefully. "But you'd better explain it to me. I mean, if it's about me and it's hurting Tom, I've got a right to know."

"I shouldn't have brought it up," Melissa said. She trailed off, and they stood together in a long, taut silence until she finally spoke again. "Some people—real jerks, you know—say Tom got you to be his campaign manager because it would make him look good up there. That that's why he won."

"Kind of a sympathy vote?" Shelley asked, her voice flat.

"It's just because Tom's so popular," Melissa plunged on. "Some people are jealous, and they say nasty stuff behind his back. Like at the beginning of the year, whenever he got permission to leave class a couple minutes early to take you somewhere, somebody'd always snicker and say he was just trying to—"

"He left class early? He asked permission?" Shelley reeled back a step, stunned. "He never told me—I never thought—"

"It was just those first few days," Melissa amended. "Listen, Tom's really wonderful, some people just can't understand anybody who's not as cloddy as they are."

"Sure," Shelley said. "Only—only what if Tom—what if the stuff they say—" She couldn't form the words that buzzed and clamored inside her head.

"Hey, Shel, don't worry about it! Please!" Melissa's voice floated to her across a bottomless chasm. "Tom really likes you! If I know anything, I know that!"

The chasm narrowed a little. "You're sure? I shouldn't be insecure, but sometimes—"

"If it were any other guy, I might wonder,"

Melissa said. "But Tom's different. You can count on him."

Yes, Shelley told herself fiercely as she hurried into the library to collect her books. Tom wasn't like anyone else. How could she think for a moment that he was exploiting her to build up his own image? He cared about her. He'd proved again and again that she could count on him. She wasn't going to let a few jealous people persuade her that it wasn't true. The cloud of doubt dissolved and floated away on a puff of happiness.

Chapter Twelve

More than ever, Shelley welcomed winter break. Besides giving her a rest from battling the crowds in the hallways, it gave her a chance to catch up on her class reading. And Kevin, who had been writing a steady stream of Braille letters, was coming to visit. Shelley knew by then that Melissa had been right about Tom. He came over every day of vacation to read to her.

"I can only read a little while today," Tom said one afternoon when he and Shelley were settled on the couch in the family room. "I've got to go over the books with the treasurer today."

"Even during Christmas vacation?" she asked. "You don't have to take your job *that* seriously, do you?"

"We'll finish the assignment, anyhow," Tom assured her, thumping the book down on the coffee table. "Besides, isn't today the day Kevin is coming up from Albuquerque?"

Shelley searched for a glimmer of jealousy in his voice, but there was none.

"Yeah," she said. "But I kind of thought you could meet each other. He's heard a lot about you."

"Well, I can probably stick around to say hello." Tom riffled through the pages of the social studies book. The cassettes of the earliest chapters had finally arrived three weeks earlier, but for some reason Mr. Jimenez had decided to leap ahead to unit sixteen.

Tom's reading was a true labor of love, Shelley reflected, settling back to listen. Tom refused to accept any payment, although the State Services for the Blind provided funds for her to spend on readers. Social studies was a pretty dreary business. When Tom read to her she never dozed off, the way she still did sometimes listening to her recorded books. He could have made the Yellow Pages sound interesting.

The doorbell chimed just as he began the section on "The Systems of Checks and Balances." "That must be him!" Shelley cried, springing up.

Tom put a restraining hand on her arm. "Watch out for the coffee table," he said. "Don't go banging your shins."

If her mom or dad had warned her about the coffee table, as if she still didn't know how to get around in her own home, she was indignant. It was one thing to be fussed over by her parents, though, and quite different to be cared about, cherished even, by a boy like Tom.

He didn't let go of her hand as they walked

together across the living room, skirting carefully around end tables and floor lamps. Marge
bounded ahead of them, and she was the
first to fling the door wide.

"Hi, is Shelley around?" Kevin began. At
the sound of Kevin's voice, as warm as ever,
sparkling with a hint of laughter, Shelley
dropped Tom's hand and flew to meet him.

For a few moments it seemed everyone was
talking at once. At last Marge's voice found
its way through the confusion. "I remember
you," she said to Kevin. "I saw you over at the
center one time when we went to visit."

"I'm sorry, I'm forgetting to introduce you
to everybody," Shelley said quickly. "Kevin,
this is my sister, Marge. And this," she ges-
tured behind her, back to where she had left
him standing, "this is Tom Travis."

"Hi. Shelley's told me about you." Tom
sounded a little formal, as if he were leading
into a speech before the junior class.

"Me, too," Kevin said. "I mean, she's told
me a lot about you."

They all giggled a little nervously over the
tangle of words.

"I'll see you guys," Marge said, edging out
of the room.

With not one, but two boys to entertain, it
was time for Shelley to act like a proper hostess. "Anybody want a Coke?" she asked. "We
can sit out on the patio if we put jackets on.
It's sunny today."

"Sure, I'm really thirsty," Kevin said. "Anything'd be great—even ice water."

"You want anything, Tom?" Shelley asked, picking up her jacket and starting toward the kitchen.

Tom overtook her in an instant. "I'll have a Coke," he said. "Don't worry, I'll get it."

He hurried into the kitchen ahead of her. He knew where the glasses were, and before she could open the cupboard he was setting them down on the counter. Shelley got the big plastic bottle of Coke from the refrigerator, but Tom took it from her without a word and filled the glasses himself.

"Do you hear from anybody at the center?" Kevin asked her from the doorway. "My dad heard this crazy rumor about Miss Chatham. Supposedly she ran off and married some guy who'd been a trainee there two years before. He's twenty years younger than she is, too."

"Miss Chatham!" Shelley exclaimed. "You're kidding! That's amazing!"

"There are potato chips in a bowl over there," Tom remarked. "Is it OK if we take them out with us?"

"Sure." She reached for the ceramic bowl that had been on the counter that morning.

"I've got it," Tom said. "Come on."

It wasn't easy to feel like a hostess, trailing after Tom through the back door to the patio. "Wait a second, I'll get you a chair," he said. Then he was beside her, offering his arm, leading her to a folding chair in the patch of afternoon sunshine.

"You ever hear anything from that roommate of yours, Bette?" Kevin asked, when they were finally settled. "I wonder how she's doing?"

"She wrote about a week ago," Shelley said. "She was in Reno, Nevada! She's motorcycling out to California with her friend Maria."

"That's perfect!" Kevin cried. "Bette on the back of a bike. I love it! What's she going to do in California?"

"She didn't have any plans," Shelley said, laughing with him. "She said it was up to the throws of the dice."

Tom cleared his throat, and she was suddenly aware how left out he must feel. What could all three of them share? Kevin couldn't care less about the finances of the junior class. And Tom wouldn't be much interested in the plans for the next Climbing Club expedition.

As she searched her mind for some neutral topic, the weather or some story in the national news, Kevin commented, "I think I passed your mother's shop, Shelley. It's the one called Regalitos, right? About a block from the plaza?"

"Yeah, that's the one."

"I just glanced in, on my way here," Kevin said. "It looked pretty quiet."

"It sure wasn't quiet last week. Marge and I went over a couple times after school to help out," Shelley said with a note of pride. Her mom had been so busy she forgot to worry about whether Shelley would knock over a shelf of vases or topple a tower of glass boxes

153

from Mexico. She was about to explain the teamwork she and Marge had developed when she heard Tom's foot tapping on the flagstone. She was losing his attention. "I've got to dash," he said. "I was the one who called this meeting. Chris'll kill me if I'm late."

"OK, then. Don't forget your book." Shelley was startled by her sense of relief. Once Tom was gone, she and Kevin could talk freely without wondering how to include Tom.

In the next moment she was stabbed by a needling thought for only a moment: shouldn't Tom have been just a little jealous of the other man in her life? Wasn't he the least bit reluctant to leave her and Kevin alone? Or didn't he think he'd have to worry about competition, since he was the only guy with enough heart to love a blind girl.

"Nice to meet you, Kevin," Tom was saying. "Maybe I'll run into you again sometime."

"Maybe so."

They were all standing now, the three of them in an uncertain little cluster, shaking hands, repeating their goodbyes. Then Tom turned away, and his tennis shoes padded around the corner of the house.

"Well," Kevin said into the silence that engulfed them. "So that's Tom."

"Yeah, that's him. Is he like you expected?"

"Yes and no."

Shelley felt suddenly awkward with her empty glass in her hand. But there was nowhere to set it down. "It's really too cold to be out here," she exclaimed. "Let's go in and get rid of the glasses and things—and then—"

"And then," Kevin supplied, "let's go for a walk."

"Hey, that's a great idea." She held out her arm for him to lead her back into the house, the way Tom always did. But Kevin hurried ahead of her across the patio. She heard a faint click as he opened the back door.

"Shelley?" he called, puzzled. "What's the matter? You coming?"

"Sure." She took a few cautious steps until she knew she must be safely past the canvas chairs. Then she relaxed and went quickly to him.

"Where are some good places to walk to around here?" he asked.

She set her glass down on the counter by the sink. "We could walk around the plaza. There are all kinds of little shops." She giggled and added, "Especially if you're in the market for beaded moccasins that'll fall apart the second time you put them on or little plaster statues that are supposed to come from some Anasazi tomb."

Kevin laughed, too. "Santa Fe's such a beautiful town," he said. "Too bad it's a tourist trap." He paused. "There must be somewhere else we can go. You've got mountains practically out your front door."

She stiffened. She hadn't been hiking since Marge had taken her. But she was ashamed to admit it to Kevin. "There's one pretty good hike I can show you," she told him. "Marge and I did it just before school started. Come on."

Out amid the traffic on Canyon Road it seemed natural enough to take Kevin's arm. They didn't talk much until the noise of civilization faded behind them, but it was a comfortable quiet. They turned onto Camino de las Estrellas, and the road grew steeper. Little by little, the scent of pine needles replaced the acrid smell of exhaust fumes. Now and then the cry of a bird dotted the steady rhythm of their tramping feet.

When they reached the giant boulder, she was almost tempted to tell Kevin about the canyon Marge had discovered. She knew she'd never be able to find it, and just telling him about it wasn't as bad as showing it to him would be. But she clamped her jaws tight on the words. Marge had shared the secret of the canyon with her, and she couldn't speak of it to anyone, not even to Kevin.

"How much farther can we go on this path?" Kevin asked. He wasn't even breathing hard.

She didn't answer for a moment, struggling to catch her breath. "It does a lot of hairpin turns up there," she said, pointing ahead of them. "Then it levels off on this nice plateau. Another half mile maybe."

They pushed on, left and right, left and right as the path snaked up the mountainside. By now they had to walk single file. Shelley followed Kevin with one hand on his shoulder. He didn't have to warn her to press close to the rough rock wall on her right. She remembered that the path there wasn't more than two feet wide, with a sheer drop on the left. Once her foot dislodged a loose stone, and it rattled down and down, skidding to rest at last at the bottom of the hideous precipice. She shuddered and hugged the wall.

"We're on the home stretch," Kevin announced. "There's one big rock to get over, then we're there."

She scrambled up the last boulder, her hands snatching at crevices, her feet clawing for toeholds. At last she sprawled, panting and laughing, on a broad, sun-warmed shelf of stone, suffused with triumph.

"I've got a box of raisins in my pocket," Kevin said. "Want some?"

Shelley nodded and heard Kevin take the box from a pocket. It was smashed and the raisins were clumped together, but they were an energy feast. Shelley sat up and leaned back against a jutting rock. The only sound was the sigh of the wind.

"It's been a mild winter so far," Kevin said. "There's snow higher up, but I would have expected some down here, too."

They were silent for a few minutes, wrapped by the stillness of the mountains. But after a while Shelley felt compelled to ask, "What did you think of Tom? You never really told me back there."

Kevin snapped a dry twig and tossed it away. "I only saw him for a few minutes," he said hesitantly. "I couldn't get much of an impression."

She had never heard him sound uncertain before. "I get the feeling you're holding something back," she said. "You must have gotten *some* kind of impression."

Kevin answered with a question. "Maybe it's none of my business, but how much time do you spend together?"

"Quite a bit. We ride back and forth to school together most days, unless he's got a meeting or something. And generally we have lunch together. We went to a party last Saturday night. And he hangs around after school sometimes, especially if there's any reading we have to do."

"Oh," Kevin said. He hesitated and asked, "Are you—you know—are you happy?"

"Of course," Shelley said, surprised. "Why shouldn't I be?"

"I don't know. I only watched you together such a short time. But it seemed like he's always doing everything for you, hovering over you—"

Shelley tensed. "He's always good to me," she said sharply. "He likes to be chivalrous, that's all. He likes to make things easier."

"Doesn't it drive you nuts, though?" Kevin pressed. "Like in the kitchen—you knew where everything was, but he wouldn't let you do a thing yourself."

"It's not that he wouldn't let me," she broke in. "He likes to help, that's all. How many guys would take the trouble to do everything he does?"

"Do you *want* him taking over for you all the time?" Kevin persisted. "When you left the center you had so much confidence. Now it seems like you're scared to walk across your own patio."

His words stung. She opened her mouth, but she couldn't answer him. She *had* left the center determined to be independent, sure she would continue to build upon everything she had learned. There were still times when she knew she was fully in charge of herself—like that afternoon at the shop last week.

"I get this weird feeling watching you, and from so much of what you've told me that he's not being good to you," Kevin plunged on. "He's stifling you! He's making you need him in ways you really don't!"

"That's ridiculous!" she burst out. "Why would he want to do that? What would he get out of it?"

"Maybe it makes him feel good," Kevin said. "Maybe he needs to feel important, somehow."

"He doesn't have to go around helping me so he can feel good," Shelley protested. "He's got lots of friends. He's involved in things; he's class president." She had made her point, she didn't have to say anything more in Tom's defense. But she couldn't stop herself as she rushed on, "You're starting to sound like some of the people who were grumbling after Tom won the election. Some of the kids who were for the guy who lost. They went around saying Tom had me give a campaign speech so people would think he's noble or something."

Kevin didn't seem to think that was absurd after all. "It's a possibility. I don't mean he's got to be evil or anything," he added hastily.

"Taking advantage of you in some sinister way. Maybe he's not even aware of what he's doing. But I bet a lot of people at your school think he's some kind of a saint. It couldn't have hurt his campaign any."

"Stop it!" she cried. "You've got no right to say that!" Tears scalded her eyes. She wanted to run away from Kevin's cruel words. But she was stuck there on that rocky plateau. He could go on talking, and she had no choice but to listen.

Kevin's voice softened. "I'm sorry," he said, edging toward her. "I shouldn't have put it that way. I only mean—"

She drew back, barely remembering to make sure there was solid ground behind her. "What do you know about it? You don't understand."

"Listen," Kevin said. "If I didn't care about you, I wouldn't bring it up. It's just that when I think how hard you worked last summer, and now I hear you saying Tom makes things easier—as if that's what you really want—it's crazy. Maybe he's not purposely using you."

But if he was, if she couldn't even count on Tom after all, how would she survive? And if there were any basis to what Kevin said, then she'd been a fool all those months, too desperate to read the warning signs.

"I'm not going to listen to this! You can talk all you want, but you can't make me listen!"

"You ought to be with a guy who'd really appreciate you and encourage you. If you'd just listen to me, give me a chance—"

"A chance!" she flung back at him. "A chance to sit here and put down the person who's helping me get my life back together? A chance to tell me I haven't lived up to some supergirl image you had of me back at the center? Don't talk to me anymore about chances!"

It was Kevin's turn to be angry. "I thought you'd at least have an open mind. You ought to be glad I was trying to be honest with you."

Shelley wrapped her arms around her knees, but she couldn't control a sudden fit of shivering.

"Let's get out of here," she said abruptly. "We've been up here long enough."

She had to hold his arm on a lot of the tricky parts going down; she didn't have any choice. Yet even when their hands touched, they might as well have been on different planets. Once Kevin tried to say something cheerful about the letters they had exchanged. She didn't answer. She scarcely heard him at all, she was working so hard to drown the echoes of the words he'd said before.

She should have known from the beginning that it would be a mistake to see Kevin again. He and his lectures belonged back there. He didn't know the first thing about the real Shelley Sayer. And now, as far as Shelley was concerned, he never would.

Chapter Thirteen

January had turned suddenly cold and buried the streets of Santa Fe beneath six inches of snow. When the plows roared through, they pushed most of the snow up onto the narrow sidewalks, making them all but impassable. Even when February's thaw turned the mounds of snow to slush, and the slush to vast muddy puddles, Shelley felt reluctant to go out alone.

"I don't blame you," Tom said sympathetically when she told him she wasn't sure she should go to an outdoor party. "It must really be hard when you don't know what you're going to step into."

"It is, kind of," she agreed. But she was still disappointed when he would go out without her instead of going over to keep her company.

"The Collected Correspondence of Kevin Burns and Shelley Sayer" was never going to fill any scholar's book. Shelley brought the shoebox down from her closet shelf one quiet Saturday morning in February and spread its contents out on her bed. She counted four fat letters, which had arrived in the fall, and then the thin, sober note she received in January. Kevin must have been practicing; his Braille was almost perfect. Slowly she unfolded the single sheet of paper and read it again.

Dear Shelley,

I've been thinking about writing to you for weeks, but it's still so hard to know how to begin. I'm really sorry I upset you so much. It's not that I want to take back anything I said. I just wish I could make you understand what I meant. It's too hard to explain it in a letter. Can we talk again sometime? I think we can still straighten it all out.

Yours always,
Kevin

He didn't apologize for one word he had said against Tom. How had he expected her to go on writing to him, talking to him on the telephone, even visiting back and forth as though nothing had changed?

She hadn't kept a copy of the letter she had typed in response, but she had agonized over it for two days and could almost remember it word for word. Leaning back against the pillow she played it over in her head:

I've thought a lot about your last letter, and I hope I can make you understand how I feel. Tom has done everything in his power to help me get back on my feet this year. He and I care for each other very much. It may seem to you that I don't have an open mind, but I know that I owe him my loyalty.

You've been a very important friend, and I miss you an awful lot. But as long as you feel the way you do about Tom, I don't think talking things over will do any good. Please, please try to understand!

There was nothing else she could have written. Without Tom her life would be empty. She would have found herself a member of the Odd Squad by October—or, even worse, she might have struggled through her days utterly alone. Instead, she was going to Melissa's party on Friday night, and on Saturday she and Marianne were going shopping for ski jackets. When she walked down the school corridors, she no longer felt like Shelley Sayer, the blind girl; she was Shelley Sayer, the girl who went with Tom Travis—accepted, respected, perhaps even envied.

She hadn't been able to forget everything Kevin had said instantly. In fact, she had gone over and over what he had said. Suppose Tom *was* only using her after all.

But using her for what? she had wondered. How could a potential Odd Squadder be of any use to a guy like Tom? If anything, *she* was exploiting *him*, taking advantage of his generosity and patience.

*   *   *

February melted into March, and March rained its way into April. Then, when there seemed no hope that spring would ever come, May exploded with bird song and fragrant blossoms, and it was unendurable to be shut up in school all day long.

Junior year was slowly drawing to a close. Tom began to talk to Shelley about running for another term as class president; after all, senior year was the only year that really mattered. But that year wasn't over yet. There were still final exams, and a class picnic, and an endless series of awards assemblies.

"It shows you what they think is really important around here," Shelley remarked to Melissa one Friday morning as they slid into their seats at the back of the auditorium. "They give awards for athletics every other week, it seems. And only one assembly all year long is for everybody else."

Melissa laughed. "It looks like half the school's up on the stage," she said. "There are about six rows of chairs."

"Who's up there that we know?" Shelley asked with interest.

"Let's see. Anna Fontaine, and Abel Tovar, naturally—he must be getting some award from the math department—and, oh, hey, there's Tom! What's he getting?"

"I don't know," Shelley said, startled. "He never said anything to me about it. I thought he'd be meeting us here."

"It must be something to do with being class president," Melissa said. "And there's Jennifer Bond and Len Moreno—"

The band struck up the "Star-Spangled Banner," cutting Melissa off in midsentence. Why hadn't Tom mentioned he was getting an award that day? Shelley wondered as her voice mingled with the ragged chorus around her. Usually he shared all of the exciting events of his days with her. Maybe he meant this to be a surprise.

As always, Mr. Higgins took full advantage of the chance to stand before the student body, and launched into a rambling speech of uninspired congratulations. Finally, reluctantly, he got down to business. First came a series of awards for "outstanding achievement in the study of a foreign language." One by one four students accepted their plaques and their share of applause. Abel Tovar received his award for mathematics, and Jennifer Bond was recognized by the music department. There were prizes for artistic achievement and awards for work in the sciences.

What had she accomplished that year? Shelley asked herself. Her B average was respectable but certainly not outstanding, and she had spent so much time struggling over homework and reading assignments that she couldn't join any after-school clubs. By senior year, at least, she'd be reading and typing faster. She wouldn't have to devote so much energy just to coping with her blindness. Maybe she'd write for the school paper or run the box office at the senior play. She'd be less absorbed with herself; she'd find ways to be involved with school again.

Yet in a sense she had achieved everything she could have hoped for that year. Her greatest accomplishment was simply sitting there, whispering and laughing with Melissa, clapping her hands when it was time to clap, blending into the crowd around her. Silently, with a smile of secret amusement, she granted herself the "ordinary person" award.

"What are you grinning about?" Melissa wanted to know, but Shelley didn't try to explain.

Ms. Standish, the drama teacher, handed out the acting awards. Mr. Suratt, who ran the Video Club, presented an award for the best film project. They'd have to get to Tom pretty soon, Shelley thought impatiently. How many people could be left up there?

"Now I'll turn the microphone over to Julie Mendez," Mr. Higgins said. "Julie?"

There was a harsh scratching sound as Julie fumbled with the mike. "Hi," she said, clearing her throat. Then she recited: "Every year the Citizens Club recognizes one among us who has made a special contribution through service to the community. This may be work within an institution, involvement with a civic organization, or service to an individual."

Had she given particular emphasis to the

words "service to an individual"? The seat squeaked as Shelley shifted uneasily.

"This year we are giving our award to someone who has been very involved with activities here at school," Julie went on. "But even more important is his exceptional service to an individual. As president of the Citizens Club, I'd like to honor Tom Travis with this plaque."

This wasn't really happening. She hadn't been listening properly. Julie must have been talking about some other individual Tom had served, not her.

She swayed forward and covered her flaming cheeks with her hands. It was all a horrible mistake. Why couldn't Julie Mendez and the Citizens Club understand that she and Tom were just one more couple walking the corridors? Tom must have been mortally embarrassed! He couldn't possibly accept an award for spending time with his girlfriend!

But the sickening swell of applause proclaimed that Tom was accepting the award. He was crossing the stage, taking the plaque in his hands . . .

The applause died away, and Mr. Higgins took over the microphone once more. But he didn't move on to the next award. He wasn't through with humiliating Shelley yet.

"Tom, this award from the Citizens Club is only a small token of the admiration we all feel for you and what you've done this year," he said, and Shelley imagined that he was shaking Tom's hand, firmly, man to man. "I think everybody here knows what we're talking about. Last year one of our students faced a real tragedy, something you and I can hardly conceive of. But she didn't let blindness stop her, she came back here in September just as if nothing had changed. Well, she's had a wonderful, generous, loyal friend this year, helping her every step of the way. And I know at this moment she must be as thrilled as I am to see Tom get his share of recognition. Shelley Sayer, will you please stand up?"

For a long, breathless second she huddled motionless in her chair, head buried in her hands. There was no room for thought in her spinning brain.

"Hey!" Melissa nudged her gently. "You're supposed to stand up."

She straightened up in her chair and pushed her hair back with a trembling hand. "No," she said dully. "I can't."

"Shelley?" Mr. Higgins repeated. "Are you out there?"

A seat creaked in the row ahead as someone twisted around to stare at her. There was nowhere to hide. And what did it matter, anyway? They had given Tom an award. They had given it, and Tom had accepted it.

The applause rolled over her like a wave as she rose to her feet. Unsmiling, wooden, she endured it for one or two interminable seconds before her legs buckled and she sank back into her seat again. If they only knew! If they could only guess that they had just snatched away the award she'd given to herself, torn it into bits, and trampled upon the pieces!

She was sure Tom would rush up to her the moment the assembly was over. He'd tell her how he had been tricked into getting up on the stage, and they'd rage together against the ignorance of Mr. Higgins and the Citizens Club and the whole school establishment. His anger would ease her pain, and when the storm abated they might even find a spark of humor in it all somewhere.

When Tom didn't appear after assembly, she consoled herself that they'd have their usual lunch together, with plenty of time to talk the whole thing out. But Tom didn't hurry up to her in the cafeteria, either. As she waited in line, her ears straining to catch his voice through the din, she remembered with a start that he had an officers' meeting. But they had social studies together in the afternoon; they'd have a minute or two to talk after class. If they could only speak for a moment she'd feel a thousand times better!

Tom breezed over to her desk as soon as the bell rang to end social studies, and her heart leaped. "Hi, Shel," he said. "I've got to run. I'll see you after school."

She couldn't deny it any longer: Tom was avoiding her. Why did he have to run? Maybe he was embarrassed that he hadn't found out about the award beforehand. If they could only talk, he could explain how the whole thing had happened. There had to be a reason he had gone through with it, something her numbed mind couldn't grasp yet. But why didn't he run to her and tell her how horrible it all was, so she could put her doubting thoughts to rest?

She scarcely heard anything her teachers said all afternoon. Her mind seethed with wrenching questions that demanded to be answered. But if Tom had no answers, what then? Then she'd know that her world had fallen to ruins, that there was nothing left.

As he did almost every day, Tom waited for her in the hall outside her eighth-period class at three o'clock. But when he greeted her, offering to carry her typewriter and a couple of her books, he made no mention of that morning's assembly. With mounting disbelief, she listened as he talked about Chris's incompetence as class treasurer: he couldn't add two and two, and it was going to take a month to get his bookkeeping ironed out. Maybe he could be impeached.

He paused at the bend in the corridor, and Shelley spoke for the first time. "I'm forgetting to congratulate you," she said, surprising herself at the iciness of her voice. "Congratulations."

"What are you talking about?" Tom asked. "Oh, that. You're not mad about that stupid award thing, are you?"

"Why should I be mad?" she heard herself ask, with the same chilly irony. "I ought to be proud of you, shouldn't I? Like Mr. Higgins said."

"Come on." Tom reached for her hand. "You can't take ridiculous stuff like that seriously!"

His hand was warm and soothing. He *would* explain, he *had* to! "Why did you go up there in the first place?" she asked, trying to keep her voice steady. "Why did you go through with it?"

They stood beside the drinking fountain, and Tom still held her hand in his. "I didn't know anything about it till last night," he began. "Julie Mendez called me around ten o'clock and said I was supposed to get to assembly a few minutes early, to be up on stage. She said I was getting some plaque from the Citizens Club, but she didn't explain what it was for, or anything."

"Didn't you ask her?" Shelley broke in.

Tom hesitated for an instant. "Well, she said something about service. But it was late, and I had a lot to do, and we didn't really get into it."

"You never suspected?" Her voice rose. She fought to bring it under control. "And then when you were up there on the stage, and they explained it all, how could you stand there and accept it? How could you?"

Tom's voice dropped to a fierce whisper, as though he didn't want to be overheard. "What was I going to do, throw that plaque in Julie's face? That'd look terrific, wouldn't it! What would people think?"

"What would people think?" she repeated.

"What did you think *I* was thinking? How could you—"

"Calm down, will you?" Tom hissed. "People are going to hear you! You're taking this all the wrong way. I don't see what you're so upset about."

"You don't? They all salute you for being my boyfriend as if you were some kind of war hero! You go along with it all, and you don't know why I'm upset?"

Tom's hand tightened around hers like a vise. She jerked free and thrust her hands behind her back.

"You want me to turn it in? Write some kind of a rejection note? How do you think that would go over?" Tom demanded. He had given up whispering by then. Anyone could have heard him halfway down the hall.

Suddenly what she *did* want rang out clear as a trumpet blast inside her head. "It wouldn't matter to me so much, your keeping the stupid thing, if you'd just feel the same way I do about it. If you'd tell me the whole thing is disgusting, and say none of it's true."

And still he didn't understand. "Say none of what's true?" he asked. "Haven't I been helping you in the cafeteria and reading to you and driving you home all year?"

"*Why* have you been doing it? That's all I care about! Tell me why."

"Why?" Tom repeated. "Have I got to spell it out? Because you can't see where the cafeteria line is, and you can't read, and you can't drive, why else? Here all the time I thought you appreciated what I was doing for you."

She couldn't speak. Her eyes were dry, the hurt was too big to ease with tears.

"I saw how people disappeared when you got out of the hospital," Tom went on. "It was pretty ugly; everybody thought so. But no one did anything. So I decided I wasn't going to be like that, too. I felt sorry for you—"

"I don't need you to feel sorry for me!" she cried. "I need you to—to like me, the way a guy likes a girl!"

"Of course I like you." Tom's answer sprang up, bright and ready for an election slogan. "You're very special to me. I don't know any other girl like you."

He was only saying words, hollow, meaningless words. How had she pretended for so long that he really cared for her? How had she ignored what Melissa said that day of the campaign speeches? *Why hadn't she listened to Kevin?*

"Shelley," Tom said, suddenly gentle. "Come on. What's the point in fighting? Let's stop at Taco Bell before I take you home, OK?"

His hand brushed her shoulder, but she backed away. She wouldn't let him touch her. "No," she said. "I'm going to take the bus."

He followed her all the way to the foyer. He talked at first, softly, persuasively, but she couldn't hear what he said. Little by little he grew silent, and his steps fell farther and farther behind. Perhaps he still watched her from a distance as she unfolded her cane and tapped across the foyer to the front door, but he didn't try to stop her.

It was easier to breathe outside, even with the exhaust fumes from the waiting school-buses. They huffed and panted at the curb, and as she stood there, trying to get her bearings, one of them pulled away with a coughing roar.

She hurried toward the nearest one, her cane tapping sharply along the pavement. "Is this number three?" she called up to the driver. "You go to Canyon Road?"

"Number three, that's me," the driver chortled. "All aboard!"

She had never used her bus pass all year, and she fumbled so long for it in her purse that the driver finally told her not to bother. Halfway down the aisle a girl said, "There's a seat over here." She staggered as the bus began to move, nearly dropping her armload of books. She couldn't be much more conspicuous, she thought. By then all eyes must have been fastened upon her. If Tom had been with her, they would have been laughing and talking, and his presence would have shielded her from the stares and whispers of the people they passed.

At last she found the empty seat. She leaned back as the bus gathered speed, waiting for the pounding of her heart to calm, for her hands to stop trembling. And then, so gradually that she couldn't have said when the first realization came, she knew that she had crossed some crucial boundary.

She was taking the bus, that was all. But no one stood by to protect her, to pave the way. She didn't need to depend on Tom or anyone else to make sure she got safely to her front door. For the first time, she was taking the bus home alone.

Chapter Fourteen

School would be out in three more weeks, and Shelley still had to write one last research paper for her English class. Once Tom would have volunteered to help her look up information in the library, but now they remained at a cool distance from each other. Shelley hired Melissa to help her with the reading she needed, paying her with money from the Services for the Blind. Melissa was happy to earn a few extra dollars, and Shelley didn't have to worry that she was exploiting her friend.

Of course nobody could read the way Tom did, but Melissa wasn't hard to listen to. The only problem was that she didn't have much endurance. After an hour of the life of Charlotte Brontë she had an uncontrollable fit of coughing and had to dash out to the drinking fountain. When she came back to their table at the back of the library, her voice was still scratchy.

"There are only ten more minutes before

the bell," Shelley said. "Maybe we can finish this tomorrow."

Melissa didn't argue. "You sure you can understand me OK?" she asked. "Sometimes my tongue gets all tangled up. I don't see why you'd want me to read to you instead of Tom."

Shelley laughed. For more than a week now, wherever she went some startled voice was bound to ask, "Hey, where's Tom?" When she left Spanish class by herself, Senora Ortiz called after her in alarm, "*Esperale tu amigo!* Wait for your friend!" Lorna caught sight of her standing in the cafeteria line and demanded, "Isn't Tom going to help you?" And each morning as she set off to catch the schoolbus, her mother asked, "Still no ride today? Where's Tom?" Sometimes it seemed that no one ever said, "Hi, Shelley," anymore. It was as if half of her were missing, and it was the half everyone had always noticed and spoken to.

"Would you want him to read to *you*," she asked Melissa, "if he thought he deserved a plaque for it?"

Melissa was silent for a long moment. "I never wanted to think it was like that," she said at last. "I kept wanting to think Tom was really just plain nice."

"You and me both," Shelley said fervently. "And he is, in his own way. Sometimes I think I expected too much. It just turned out he didn't feel about me the way I wished he would—the way I felt about him."

"You don't think he was using you, the way

178

Len Moreno and those guys said?" Melissa asked.

Shelley sighed. "I don't know if I'll ever sort it all out," she said. "Maybe he was without quite knowing it himself. Could that be? I think basically he did mean well, at least most of the time."

"So many of the guys around here are such creeps, when you come down to it," Melissa said sadly. "When I'd see Tom with you, it kind of kept my hopes up. I wanted to think he was different."

"He is different," Shelley said. She twisted the strap of her pocketbook between her fingers. "The other guys I used to go out with haven't beaten a path to my door. Maybe nobody but Tom—"

She couldn't finish the thought out loud. It would sound self-pitying, and Melissa would feel obligated to reassure her. But she wasn't pitying herself. She was trying to be realistic, to face the truth she'd been hiding from all those months. Maybe the only boys who would ever want her would feel sorry for her, would need to be needed, would want to be seen as noble martyrs. Maybe she would never meet anyone who saw her as an interesting, attractive girl, someone who could take as well as give.

"My mother says the guys grow up a little once they get to college," Melissa was saying. "It's something to look forward to, anyway."

"A few of them are OK, even in high school," Shelley said, to her own surprise. "I had a friend, Kevin, the son of one of the trainees at the center. But I didn't know how special he was."

"Kevin?" Melissa asked. "Hey, you never told me about him."

High heels clicked sharply toward them between the rows of nearly empty tables. "Are you girls still working, or are you just visiting?" demanded Ms. Pauling, the librarian.

"Well," Shelley began, "we were just—" But already Ms. Pauling was clicking back the way she had come.

Shelley used the interruption to avoid Melissa's comment about Kevin. What was the use in talking about him or even thinking about him now? He had been her friend, and he had tried to tell her what he thought she ought to hear. But after the way she had treated him, he'd never want to speak to her again.

The house was quiet when she let herself in the front door, and for the first few moments Shelley thought she was alone. Then through the kitchen window floated the uneven rasping of a saw.

"Marge?" she called, stepping onto the patio. "What in the world are you doing?"

"I'm building a bookcase to put my china horse collection on," Marge said with a ring of pride. She paused and added a little uncertainly, "I'm trying to, anyway."

Shelley started toward her. Her foot rattled against a piece of wood, and she bent to inspect a pile of lumber, all rough boards of odd shapes and sizes.

"It's all scraps from out in the toolshed," Marge said. "Nobody else is ever going to use it. I asked Dad if I could make something for my room, but he thinks I'll cut my foot off."

"You're not using the power saw," Shelley said. "What makes him think—"

Marge sighed. "*You* know how Dad is."

She knew, all right. But she hadn't realized that Marge felt the same way. "He's got too good an imagination," Shelley said, squatting on the flagstones. "Like if I say I'm going to walk to the plaza, he right away pictures this Mack truck roaring along out of control down Canyon Road, running up onto the sidewalk, and wiping me out. It's a fact before I'm even out the door."

"Mom goes right along with him," Marge said. "You sure can see why the two of them got together."

"Did he actually say you couldn't try to build something?" Shelley asked.

"He thought he had talked me out of it," Marge said. "After warning me about all the things that could go wrong he figured he didn't have to bother saying no."

Shelley examined the two narrow side pieces, joined at the top and the bottom to form a shaky oblong frame.

"I should have cut all the shelves first," Marge said ruefully. "I started putting the next one in but it's too long, so I'm sawing it a little shorter."

"Somebody'll see the sawdust," Shelley pointed out.

"I'll clean it up. I'm being real careful." Marge stood up, and there was a thud as she jumped over a stray board. "I'm starving," she said over her shoulder. "Time for a break."

Shelley scrambled up and followed her inside. "Any mail?" she asked, trying to keep her tone casual.

Her heart quickened with hope when Marge said, "Yeah, there's something for you." Maybe Kevin had decided to give her another chance. Maybe they could resume the "Collected Correspondence" after all. But she could tell by the lean smooth envelope that there were no Braille pages folded inside. "It's from the Climbing Club," Marge told her. "Looks like a newsletter. Let's see, 'New officers for the Northeast New Mexico chapter . . . lecture and slides on mountain wildlife June thirteenth . . . fund-raising dinner July tenth . . .' "

Shelley ought to have told Marge not to bother reading any further. All year she had been tossing Climbing Club notices into the wastebasket. Yet she didn't interrupt as Marge read on.

" 'A talk on the threat to the American grizzly . . . join the climb of Capital Peak—' "

"When's that?" Shelley asked.

Marge read the announcement through. " 'Some places are still available for club members who wish to join the climb of Capital peak in southern Colorado. This majestic peak is noted for its spectacular scenery. While most of its trails are accessible to beginners, Capital also offers challenges for the experienced rock climber. Registration fees must be received by May twenty-seventh. The group will convene in the parking lot of club headquarters in Albuquerque at five AM on July sixth.' "

Even as she told herself that the idea was ridiculous, Shelley leaned forward to absorb every word. Whcn Marge handed the newsletter back at last, Shelley sat in silence, folding and unfolding the crisp pages.

"Just think what Dad's imagination would come up with if I ever signed up for a real climb," she said. "Avalanches. Landslides. Rabid bears."

"You're sure Capital Peak isn't a volcano?" Marge put in, giggling. "Just as you get to the top it'll blow like Mount Saint Helens."

In an instant all of the humor evaporated. "I didn't say I was going to the top," Shelley said. "I was just thinking, you know."

"Yeah." Marge opened the refrigerator. "Yuck! There's nothing in here but Mom's diet ginger ale. You want any?"

"No thanks." Shelley propped her elbow on the table and rested her chin in her hand. Behind her Marge clattered about, dropping ice cubes into a glass and banging drawers open and shut, before she finally came back to the table.

Marge thumped a book down in front of her and leafed through its pages as she sipped her ginger ale. Shelley sat motionless, but in her mind she was flying, rappelling down a sheer cliff face as yard after yard of rope played out from the cleat at her belt. She could almost feel the wind whipping her cheeks, the roughness of rock against the soles of her boots. She had always wanted to climb Capital Peak, ever since she watched a video about a team that tackled it. She was still a club member, still eligible if she mailed in her registration fee on time.

Eligible, sure! taunted a voice inside her head. She could register, but what good would she be on a climbing team? She'd be in everyone's way, a dead weight dragging down the whole expedition. She had even stumbled and fallen on that mild little walk with Marge in September. How could she think of Capital Peak for three seconds?

"There's a picture here of the bookcase I'm making," Marge said. "It's going to be fantastic. Dad'll flip out when he sees it."

"How many more afternoons will it take you?" Shelley asked suddenly. She didn't wait for an answer. "You think if you go out for any hikes around here—would you mind if I came with you once in a while? I'm so out of shape it's disgusting."

Marge shut her book with a snap. "What do you mean, would I mind?" she demanded. "It'd be fun, if you really want to come with me."

"I do," Shelley said. "None of the mountains around here have real cliffs where you need ropes and all that. But I want to get as much practice as I can. I haven't been out there in so long."

It wouldn't hurt to get outdoors again, and Marge would be patient, even if everything took her three times as long as it ought to. It still didn't mean that she had to sign up for the climb.

Marge pushed back her chair. "I better pound another couple nails in," she said. "I've still got to sweep up before the folks come home."

"I'll be out in a minute," Shelley said, walking with her to the door.

In a few moments the saw rasped across the quiet of the afternoon once more. "Yow-ee!" Marge hollered, laughing. "There goes my left foot!"

If Shelley wanted to risk breaking her neck on Capital Peak, there was no reason to discuss her decision with Kevin. It was true he had urged her to climb again, even suggested that they might climb together one day. But that was long ago and he had probably forgotten by then. She had been so cold and hurtful to him, in person and then through her letter, that he probably wanted nothing more to do with her.

Shelley paced across the kitchen, through the living room to the front door. She leaned there, immobile against a torrent of thoughts. She wasn't really the helpless, fragile creature Tom had imagined her, capable of doing a few things for herself, but always in need of protection. Acquiescing, molding herself into the girl he thought she should be, she had given away an essential part of who she was. Tom had betrayed her in the end, but really it was she who had betrayed herself.

She had mastered all of Miss Chatham's "activities of daily living." She seldom agonized anymore about eating spaghetti in public or went into a cold panic thinking she had somehow put on one brown shoe and one black. She was ready to face a real challenge, to attempt something wonderful and exciting. If she were ever to return to the mountains, the time was now. And it would seem wrong somehow to sign up for the Capital Peak climb without telling Kevin.

She'd explain everything. She'd apologize for the way she had treated him and tell him he was right about Tom all along. Kevin wasn't the sort of guy who'd hold a grudge. Everything between them would be all right again, and perhaps they could be friends as they had been before.

She had almost reached the phone when another thought jolted her to a stop. What was she going to say? "Hi, Kevin, Tom and I broke up, so I thought I'd give you a call!" He'd figure that since things hadn't worked out with Tom, she was looking for a substitute.

It wasn't the sort of thing she could talk about over the phone. But, perhaps, if she met him face to face, she could make him understand. What Kevin thought of her, the way he felt about her, mattered more than she could bear. She finally had to admit that if Kevin's opinion hadn't meant so much to her, his words wouldn't have stung her the way they had.

She reached for the phone and dialed.

An unfamiliar woman's voice answered, and for a moment she believed she had punched an incorrect digit somewhere. "Is Kevin there?" she asked. "Kevin Burns?"

But the woman had to be Kevin's mother. Her voice was distorted as she covered the mouthpiece and called, "Kevin! Phone!"

She could still hang up. She hadn't said her name. He would never know—

"Hello?" Kevin's voice in her ear was just the same, as warm and welcoming as if he had called to her across the lounge at the center. Her breath caught in her throat and for a moment she couldn't speak.

"Hello?" Kevin repeated. "Who is this?"

"Kevin? It's me. Shelley."

It was Kevin's turn to be silent. She pictured the wires that spanned the yawning distance between them. High tension wires—

"Shelley." Just her name, then the silence hummed along the circuits again.

"Yeah, hi," she said stupidly. "How are you? How's everything going?"

"OK, I guess. Shelley, what's going on with you?"

He wasn't simply making small talk. He wanted to know what she was doing on the other end of the line, why after all these months she had chosen to turn up in his life again.

She had to say something. The silence was unendurable. With no more pretense at small talk, she plunged straight in. "I got the Climbing Club newsletter today. Did you? There's a climb on Capital Peak the first weekend in July."

"Oh, yeah?" Kevin still kept his tone noncommittal, forcing her to go on.

"I was thinking," she floundered. "Remember one time you said you thought I should try climbing again? Well, I guess I'm going to sign up."

"You are?" he cried, and she knew she wasn't imagining the delight in his voice. "That's great! You'll find, once you get started, you can do so much of it by feel. I've seen pictures of Capital, it's beautiful!"

Slowly she relaxed, leaning back against the wall. "I've been missing the mountains for so long," she said. "Maybe I'm nuts, but I'm going to do it." She hesitated. "Are you?"

"Do you want me to?" Kevin asked, and once more his voice was tense.

Shelley hesitated. If she wanted him to go on the climb with her, she'd have to explain everything right now. But she couldn't arrange the words. When she opened her mouth it was going to come out all wrong.

"Maybe it'd be better if I don't," Kevin was saying. "I mean, considering everything, do you want me to sign up?"

All she could manage was a fervent whisper, "Yes!"

"OK," Kevin said. "I'll do it."

She was giddy with excitement when she hung up the phone. She'd have to register right away, before the last few places were filled. Of course it would be a battle, persuading her dad to sign the permission forms, but she'd talk him into it somehow. She'd have to dig her climbing gear out of the closet, figure out if she needed to buy anything new. She could do push-ups and sit-ups on her own, and go for plenty of walks with Marge, too. She still had more than a month to get into shape. She'd prove to herself that when she wanted to do something badly enough, she could find a way.

Outside, Marge's hammer banged out a staccato rhythm. Shelley opened the cleaning closet, releasing a tumble of rags and sponges. The broom poked out at her right away, but the dustpan was so well buried she almost didn't find it at all. At last she clattered over to the back door. "You finished with the sawing part?" she called. "I'll help you conceal the evidence."

Chapter Fifteen

"Just thought I'd drop by," Tom said from the open door. "I thought maybe we could talk."

Shelley had never heard him sound so hesitant. They had been politely distant through the final weeks of school, though even the sound of his voice across a crowded room still wrenched her with pain and anger. And now there he was, stammering in the doorway.

"Come on in," she said, stepping aside. "My folks are on the patio; we can sit in the family room."

She half expected him to thrust out a restraining hand as she stepped between the hassock and the lamp, but he didn't touch her. Trailing after her, he was unnaturally quiet. He had stayed away ever since the day of the awards assembly. What had brought him there then, on the afternoon before the Capital Peak climb?

She sat down across the room from him and leaned back, working to look relaxed.

But her heart thudded as she asked, "Well, what's up?" Maybe he understood at last, maybe he'd come to say he wanted to make a fresh start.

"Oh, nothing much," Tom said. Something in his tone told her that he was struggling to sound casual, too. "I was just, you know, in the neighborhood."

"Oh," she said. She lifted a little ceramic bird from the end table beside her and turned it between her hands. Tom hadn't just dropped over on a whim. He had come with a definite purpose, and if she was patient she would learn what it was.

"I ran into Melissa yesterday," Tom said abruptly. "She was telling me you're going to go mountain climbing or something."

"Tomorrow," she said. "Mom's driving me down to Albuquerque tonight."

"You really *are* doing it, then?" Tom asked. "I thought Melissa had it mixed up. You know how she is about details sometimes."

Shelley tensed. He was saying that there had to be some mistake, that he didn't believe she could really go climbing. "I've still got to get my backpack ready," she said. "It's been fun, pulling out all my equipment again. It's been so long since I had my hands on carabiner clips and hexentrics and—"

"How are you going to manage it?" Tom broke in. "It's dangerous. People get killed every year."

She had argued it with her father for a week before he finally gave in. Now here it was all over again. "Most of it's just straight hiking," she explained. "And when you get into real rock climbing, finding toeholds, testing whether your rope will hold, most of that stuff you can do by feel."

"It doesn't make sense," Tom exclaimed. "You wouldn't catch me hanging by a rope off a cliff, and I can see where I'm going to fall."

"You haven't ever been climbing. I've had some experience, not a whole lot, not like some climbers I've met, but some. When I really think about it, I know I can do it."

Tom was silent, and for a moment she thought he was ready to let the subject drop. Then he began on a different tack. "Every time I think about you crawling around up there, I get this awful feeling you're trying to prove something. Trying to prove something to me."

"What?" Stunned, she jerked upright on her chair. The ceramic bird fell to her lap.

"From some of the things you said that day," Tom went on, "I got the feeling that somehow you felt that I was holding you back, not letting you be independent, right? So now you're going to take your life in your hands just to show me what you can do."

"That's crazy! I wouldn't do something I didn't want to do, just to make an impression on you." Had she ever really been so lost? She knew that once he had mattered so much she would have done almost anything to become the girl he wanted. But the last thing Tom wanted was a girl—especially a blind girl—who headed off to climb mountains.

Tom didn't seem to hear her. "You don't have to prove anything to me," he said. "If you get hurt—"

"If I get hurt it won't be your fault," Shelley declared. "Ever since I went blind I've missed mountain climbing so much. For a long time I was afraid I'd have to give it up. But it's part of me, you know? It took me all this time to get up the guts to go back and try again." If he really cared for her, he'd understand. He'd cheer her on and revive her own flagging courage.

"Come on," Tom pleaded. "Don't get me wrong, I'm not saying you've got to be an invalid. But you try to be *too* independent. Some things—you know, you've got to be realistic."

"I *am* being realistic. Once I get past being scared that I'll slip and slide and make a fool of myself up there, I know I can do it."

Shelley stood up. "I've got to leave in two hours, and I still have a zillion things to do."

There was no point talking any more about climbing or anything else. Tom stood up silently, and Shelley walked him to the door. As the door closed behind him, she felt a bittersweet sense of relief. She had decieved herself for so long, telling herself that Tom was the boy she wanted. Now she was free of him at last.

But suppose the only boys who would ever look at her *were* people like Tom, boys who wanted her to be helpless and dependent on them for everything? Well, if that were the case, she'd just have to get used to being alone.

Slowly she went to her room to pack. Stretching up on tiptoe, she slid her nylon backpack, jingling with dangling straps, down from her top closet shelf. It was like a faithful old friend, with all its familiar pouches and latches. She thought of all the climbs they had weathered together. It had carried clothes and bedroll and pup tent, camera and notebook for recording the scenery and her thoughts. And it had softened one or two falls that could have been disastrous without all that padding to land on.

The next day she would be out on the peaks again, with her pack strapped to her back. The next day she would know for certain whether she could still climb to the windswept heights she had always loved.

After her parents dropped her off, Shelley spent the night—what there was of it—with a half dozen other out-of-towners in the Climbing Club's lodge in Albuquerque. Kevin and those who lived close by wouldn't arrive until morning. She knew she should get as much sleep as possible, that she'd need to be totally alert in the morning. But for a long time she lay awake on the lower bunk, her mind racing to the day ahead. She had been arguing with other people for so long that she hadn't had time for her own doubts and fears to surface. Now they swarmed in on her like a pack of demons. Kevin would be watching her, expecting her to climb as she had two years earlier. But suppose she was so slow she ruined the climb for everyone else? Suppose she fell and had to be hauled out of a crevasse? Suppose she made a fool of herself in front of the whole team? She should have stayed safe and quiet at home. Perhaps, after all, she was being unrealistic!

At four-thirty she staggered out of bed to a recording of "Reveille" that blared from speakers in the hall. It seemed ridiculous to get up that early when they would be driving past Santa Fe later. But Albuquerque was the point of origin for the trip. A mug of scalding black coffee in the dining room helped clear the sleep from her head, but she still felt a little dazed. People seemed to speak from a long way off, and the edges of their words were muted and blurry. Even as she walked with the others to the parking lot, the sharp air burning her cheeks, she felt she was moving through a dream.

She jolted fully awake when Kevin said softly beside her, "Hi. Looks like we both made it."

What was the matter with her? Her heart never used to lurch like that when Kevin spoke to her back at the center. "I'm really going through with this," she said with a tense little laugh. "I've been thinking about it so much I can't believe it's going to happen."

"I always think it's a drag getting up in the middle of the night," Kevin remarked. "But then, once you're outside, there's something special about the air."

"Until about eight in the morning," Shelley agreed. "It's so still. And even here in the city it smells clean, as if night gives the air a chance to revive."

Kevin had a way of getting her to say things she had never put into words before. He was such a good friend. How had she ever said all those terrible things to him that afternoon when he came to visit? Even now he must be remembering, thinking about what a petty, mean-spirited person she really was.

"Kevin, I've got to talk to you!" she said in a rush. "I've got to explain—"

"What?" he asked. His tone was neutral, waiting.

People chattered all around them, comparing equipment, reminiscing about other climbs, planning the day ahead. Shelley stepped away from the crowd, drawing Kevin into a space apart. "When I got your letter," she said, her voice low and hurried, "I should have called you. You were right about Tom. You were right about everything."

"How do you mean?" Kevin asked.

"When you said he was, you know, stifling me—" It was hard to get the words out. Even then it still hurt her a little, reminding herself that it was true. "I don't think he did it on purpose, exactly. Partly he really meant to help me. But after a while it kind of fell apart."

Anyone else might have exclaimed in triumph, "I told you so! You shouuld have listened to me!" But for a long moment Kevin was silent, while she waited, her hands clenched at her sides.

"I ought to be sorry, I guess," he said at last. "I mean, it must have been pretty awful breaking up, when you were counting on him and all." He stepped nearer, and his hand brushed her arm. "Only maybe it's just as well you got free of him. At least you're here now, and I—we—"

But as she waited for him to go on, scarcely breathing, she sensed that he was suddenly distracted. Eager voices clamored, and there was a shift in the crowd, an excited movement forward. "This is it!" one of the boys cried. "Here comes the van!" "Hey, hey," shouted a girl close by. "We're going to Colorado!"

"I guess this isn't exactly the right time to talk," Kevin sighed. "But later. There's still a lot to say, I think." He wasn't angry! He was— she searched for words to define it to herself— so much more than forgiving! "Later," she repeated to herself. He had said it as a promise.

The van rattled to a stop a few yards away, and the door clanged open. "Morning, folks," called a brisk, cheerful voice. "I'm Steve Bristow; you can call me Steve. I'll be your guide up to Capital Peak today. I assume this *is* the Capital Peak team, isn't it?"

There was a little ripple of laughter. They all edged closer to the van, ready to scramble aboard and be off. It would be warm inside, fragrant with the smell of oiled boots and coils of rope, and after they had gone thirty miles and begun to feel as if they really were a team, maybe someone would start a song.

"Let me just go down my list, make sure we're not missing anybody," Steve Bristow said. Shelley painted his portrait in her mind: he was thirtyish, with wild dark hair and a beard, bright eyes smiling from a face craggy as the mountains he knew so well, "As I call your name, climb in and grab a seat. Cheryl Amado, Terry Blair . . ."

Shelley gripped the strap of her pack until it bit into her palm. It was too late to change her mind now. And with a surge of anticipation she knew she wanted to do this climb more than she had wanted anything in a very long time. In only four more hours she'd feel the rocks of the trail under her feet, and the mountain wind in her hair.

"Kevin Burns," Steve called, and Kevin slipped from her side. "Stella Mat—Mat—Matijevich? Shelley Sayer?"

Tapping her cane before her, Shelley followed the sound of Stella Matijevich's footsteps to the door of the van. She hoped Kevin had saved her a place. Even if there was no privacy for them to talk, it would be good to share the trip with him, to have him close beside her.

"Shelley Sayer?" Steve's voice was sharp with surprise—or was it annoyance?

She stopped short, the tip of her cane touching the van's front tire. "That's me," she said. "I'm Shelley."

The silence stretched taut through one shivering moment, then another. "Wait a minute. It doesn't say anything here about—about—" He floundered helplessly.

"About my being blind?" Shelley filled in. Once he heard the word, once he saw she wasn't afraid of it, he'd probably feel more comfortable with it.

It didn't work. "This is a mountain-climbing group," he said persuasively, as though he were talking to a bewildered child. "We're going up to fourteen thousand feet today, we're going to do some rugged rock climbing—"

"I know," Shelley said. "I belong to the Climbing Club. This is my seventh climb." Her words were steady, but her body was turning to jelly. For weeks she had thought her biggest hurdle would be to convince her father to sign the permission form. Why hadn't she realized that she had to face a complete stranger who had the power to refuse her, to put her and her backpack on the next bus back to Santa Fe?

"Your seventh?" Steve repeated, astounded. Shelley held her breath. She wasn't about to volunteer that she had been able to see when she made those other six climbs. But if he asked her, she couldn't very well lie about it, either.

Behind her she heard the impatient stamping of boots. She was holding up the whole expedition already, and they hadn't even left the parking lot. "Listen, I'm sorry, but I just haven't got the training for this kind of thing," Steve said gently. "Maybe if there were two guides it could work. But I've got ten climbers in this group, and I won't have time to be responsible for you."

Her toeholds were giving way. She was sliding into a fall, with no rope to save her. Would he drop her off at the bus station or call a taxi while the others waited in the van, muttering about the time being lost? "But I've had more experience than a lot of other people here," she cried. "If somebody just hollers directions once in a while, I can follow the trail. Give me a chance, OK?"

Even as she spoke, she knew her words didn't reach him. Her experience, her simple explanation of how she would manage on the climb—nothing counted for Steve beyond her blindness. She braced herself to accept his answer with a shred of dignity. Cushioned with apologies, sweetened with admiration for her courage, it would still be the same irrevocable *no*.

"She's not kidding. You ought to see her. I've climbed with her before, and she can do anything!" Kevin spoke from above, leaning from the window of the van. Somehow the added height gave his voice a ring of authority.

"You've seen her climb?" Steve asked. "I can't picture it. How on earth—"

"I guess she mostly puts one foot in front of the other," Kevin said. "Right, Shelley?"

"Something like that," she stammered. "It's

not as hard as you think, once you get used to it."

"Listen," Steve told Kevin. "You've worked with her before—maybe you could keep an eye on her out there, you know? Kind of be her guide, on a one-to-one."

"Sure," Kevin said. "Come on up, Shelley. There's an empty seat here next to me."

Her legs trembled as she clambered up into the van. Half stumbling over someone's pack on the floor, she flopped into the seat beside Kevin. Through a fog she heard Steve call out the last names. Then the laughter and talk around her were lost to the swelling roar of the motor. "We're off!" someone shouted, and the van surged forward on the first lap of the journey.

"Thanks," she said, leaning toward Kevin. "You saved my life!"

"I wasn't going to sit there and let him send you home, was I?" Kevin asked.

But why had Steve only heard what Kevin was saying? Shelley wondered. Why hadn't he listened to her in the first place?

Perhaps he shouldn't have listened to either of them. He had agreed to take Shelley on this climb under false pretexts. "Kevin," she said close to Kevin's ear, hoping he'd catch her words above the noise of the van. "You never saw me climb. I mean, you haven't ever seen me climb *blind*. What if—"

Kevin's hand, cool and firm, folded over hers. "I didn't say anything that wasn't true," he murmured. "You were terrific when I saw you, and you're going to be great today. If *you* don't know it, *I* do."

The van was quiet for a while, and Shelley let her mind wander as it climbed slowly away from Albuquerque, pushing north past Santa Fe and into the mountains. As the warmth from the sun touched her cheek, one of the girls began to sing "You Are My Sunshine." When some of the others joined in, Shelley found herself singing, too. Their voices blended exuberantly as the highway swept them along. Shelley was just another member of the team. All together they were going to scale Capital Peak.

Chapter Sixteen

Even by nine o'clock, when the Climbing Club expedition finally embarked on the first lap of the climb, a swarm of tourists already clattered about on the lower trail. But their shouts and laughter and the spasmodic clicking of cameras didn't rob Shelley of that first rush of excitement. When she reached the end of the paved walk beyond the park office and stepped onto the pounded dirt of the path, she knew with a rush of joy that she would be climbing again soon.

The going was easy for an hour or more, and when Kevin asked if she wanted to take his arm, she shook her head. Tapping her cane before her, she had no trouble keeping to the path. She reveled in the sense of freedom, moving at her own pace, each step carrying her deeper into adventure.

The trail rose gradually for a time, broad and smooth and well traveled. Then it suddenly leveled off for a dozen yards before Shelley found herself at the foot of a flight of rough stone stairs. "There's even a railing," Kevin called to her over his shoulder. "On your right."

"How civilized!" she said and giggled. "Super-Climber would love it!"

"No, too rough," Kevin said. "He'd rather install an escalator."

Behind her the voice of a middle-aged female tourist wailed, "I don't know if my feet can take this! Oh, my fallen arches!" No wonder serious climbers made fun of tourists, Shelley thought, and she felt a glow of pride that her boots and pack set her apart. But she really couldn't mock beginners. She had already fallen to the rear of the climbing party, and now the distance between the others and her seemed to be widening.

She quickened her steps, gripping the iron rail when she almost stumbled over an unexpected turn. From up ahead she caught a snatch of Steve's words, "Plenty of guts, anyhow . . . got to give her credit . . ." A flush of shame crept up her cheeks. *Guts!* Because she mounted a simple set of stairs that any self-respecting climber would sneer at, she had to be given credit! She'd show Steve Bristow that she was in a different league from that moaning tourist with the fallen arches!

After the stairs the trail was steeper, broken here and there by jutting rocks. Once her cane tangled in a mass of prickly undergrowth. By the time she pulled it loose and found the path again, the voices of the others were fading far ahead. The trail was getting rougher all the time; she'd never catch up with them now. If she lost the path she might wander for hours before anyone found her. And Steve and her father and Tom would all say they had warned her that blind girls weren't capable of climbing mountains.

Keep calm, she told herself harshly. *Keep moving, slow, steady, forward!*

"Shelley, you want to take my arm? It gets a little tricky up here!" Kevin said from only a few yards away.

He sounded so natural and unruffled that she laughed at her own fright. "I know I couldn't go it alone forever," she told him, catching up. "I guess this is it."

She folded her cane and slipped it into her backpack. Tucking her hand into the crook of Kevin's arm, she followed him easily up and over rocks and around hairpin twists in the path. Within a few minutes they were with the others again.

"First milestone's coming up," Steve announced. "This little lean-to on the right marks the end of the two-mile hiking path. We'll take a ten-minute break."

"Here's where we separate the men from the boys. Right, Stella?" one of the guys asked, laughing.

"Sexist! How about the women from the girls!" Stella protested.

"Let's check out the lean-to," Kevin said, and several of the others crowded in behind them. "Hey, look. There's a book you can sign."

" 'The Park Service welcomes the comments and suggestions of visitors to Capital Peak,' " Steve read aloud at Shelley's elbow. " 'We hope your experience has been a safe and pleasant one.' That's for all the folks who aren't going any farther."

Kevin's pen scratched for a few seconds upon the page. At last he turned and read, " 'Comments: We had a terrific time on the lower trail, except for when the mountain lions ambushed us. Please send a ranger to track my partner. He was last seen wrestling a cougar over the edge of a cliff. I may be forced to file charges of hiker abuse.' "

Shelley laughed, and beside her Steve chuckled, too. But in another minute he was all brisk business again. "This next section is still straight hiking," he explained when he called the group together. "But it starts getting pretty steep. We want to keep moving at a good clip so we can reach our campsite by two o'clock. We'll stop there just long enough on our way up to drop off a lot of our gear. That way we can travel light to the top."

A sigh of relief swept the circle before he went on: "We've really got to keep moving if we want to reach the top and make it back to base camp before sundown. We'll get into some real cliff climbing after we lighten the packs. There's one stretch that's about as close to perpendicular as you're ever going to come, unless you're reincarnated as a lizard."

206

They put on their helmets before they set off again. "I'm not going to think ahead," Shelley said, tightening her chin strap. "One step at a time, right?"

"It's going to be single file from now on," Kevin told her, turning to study the trail. "Maybe you can put your hand on my back-pack and follow me like that."

There was a special feeling about hiking with a team. No one spoke much, as if they were all conserving their strength for what was to come. Yet Shelley was keenly aware of the others around her, through the crunch of pebbles under booted feet and the jingle of carabiner clips on belts. And always Kevin walked just a step ahead, calmly, steadily leading the way.

Once a yell and a scuffling, scrambling noise at the front of the group punctuated the silence. "Cheryl just fell," Kevin informed her. "She kind of skidded and lost her balance. There's a really rough spot coming up."

Only a few moments later Steve gave a warning shout, "Rock!" from the head of the procession, and Shelley flung herself facedown on the ground as the boulder leaped and crashed past her, hurtling toward the valley below. It was a big one, from the sound of it. She shuddered, wondering what real protection a helmet would offer if a stone like that bounced off her head.

As the sun blazed hotter, the climb grew steeper and more rugged. With satisfaction Shelley noticed that she still breathed easily despite the altitude and the exertion, and her feet instinctively found niches in the rock. Perhaps some of those practice trips with Marge were paying off. For the most part, that phase of the climb hadn't been much harder than the hiking they had done around Santa Fe. Her thoughts leaned toward Kevin as her hand rested on the top of his pack. Did he find it impossible not to think about her? What would he say to her later when the climb was over? If it ever *was* over, if she survived that perpendicular Steve warned them about.

"Here's where we'll make camp tonight," Steve told the group when they reached a smooth plateau. "We can drop off our tents and bedrolls."

There was a general sigh of relief before he went on, "Believe it or not, we're going up that cliff over there, straight to the top."

Amid the mingled groans and whoops of amazement, Shelley asked Kevin, "Is it all that bad?"

"Well," he said, "I can see two easy parts. But the rest of it—it'd be great for a human fly. And way up there, there's still a good bit of snow."

Shelley crouched and drew a thick coil of rope from her pack. Her hands shook as she threaded it through the climbing harness she wore around her hips and waist, pulling the knots tight. Digging deeper into her pack, she unearthed a clanking assortment of "protections": metal wedges of various shapes and sizes which could be tied to the rope and lodged into cracks to secure her hold. At home as she had caressed and studied each one, she had set it into a crevice in her imagination, strung the rope through its holes, and glided gracefully up to the next handhold. Now the oddly irregular "stops" and "hexentrics" filled her with trembling dread. She had always gone through a bit of last-minute panic when she contemplated a cliff face, she reminded herself. This time wasn't so very different.

But Shelley's anxiety only grew. What was she doing on top of a mountain, anyway? She was *blind*—the truth struck her with all the force of that long-ago afternoon when she arrived at the center in Albuquerque. What had possessed her to believe she could find her way up a cliff that she couldn't even see?

"Everybody set?" Steve was approaching, pausing to inspect each climber along the way. He laughed with Kevin over the complicated set of knots Kevin was tying, and made some joke about sailors in the rigging, which Shelley was too nervous to grasp.

Then he stepped to her side, and she felt his gaze upon her, curious and uncertain. "You really amaze me," he said. "I don't think I could do what you've done today." As she fumbled for a response he continued, "You know, there's an easier way to do this final stretch. The same trail we've been on loops around and up. Somebody could take you that way, and you might even be at the top before the rest of us."

In an instant Shelley was on her feet, her confidence found again and all her fears swept aside. "No, thanks," she said firmly. "I want to do this. I want the challenge."

"If you say so," Steve said. Shelley pictured him shaking his head, a look of dismay and bewilderment chasing across his face before he moved to the next climber.

Crossing the narrow plateau, she felt the precipice towering above her, ancient and immense. When she could see, she had stood at the foot of cliffs like that one, studying their jagged patterns of pits and creases until she had mapped out a route to take. She played a game with a silent opponent—the mountain, master of a thousand secrets. She looked up at the mountain and knew that if she were clever, and very patient, she would reach heights where only a privileged few had ever stood before.

Now she stretched on tiptoe, searching upward as high as she could reach for holds. But even as she set her foot into a groove and started to haul herself up, she knew it wasn't going to work. She might climb thirty feet and find herself at a dead end.

Already Steve and two or three of the others had begun. "Kevin?" she asked. "You think you could go ahead of me and kind of give me some directions?"

"I figure that's the most logical way to work

it," Kevin said. "I'm watching Steve. We can follow in his footsteps, as it were."

"As it were," Shelley repeated, laughing with relief. She had been half afraid that by asking for help she was admitting that she really couldn't handle the climb after all. But Kevin was right—the others were all watching Steve, too, as he charted a course for them to follow. The only difference for Shelley was that Kevin would translate that into words before she followed it.

"OK," Kevin began. "There's a ledge about knee high where you can put your right foot. There, now reach with your left hand and grab that little knob, there, that one. Pull yourself up to the ledge that's just above your right hand. Now, just above your shoulder there's a good deep crack where you can wedge in a stop."

Slowly, gingerly at first, Shelley clambered higher and higher. The past and the future melted away, and her whole being concentrated upon the sliver of time that was now, the place that was there—a crevice, the next toehold, the reassuring tug of the rope at her waist. Soon her hands seized upon holds even before Kevin could tell her where to find them. The gap between her and the others was widening again, but she didn't care. Her feet grappled over the rock, her hands read its every bump and furrow. Kevin's boots grated above her, but he spoke less and less often now. She followed the jingle of clips on his belt, but from moment to moment she was discovering her own way.

The sun shone less intensely now, and Shelley knew that the afternoon was slipping away. There were the two relatively easy stretches Kevin had foreseen, places where the rocks sloped at a generous angle and they could walk almost normally. Her foot slipped eventually beneath an overhanging stone into something soft and powdery and she bent down to find her first patch of snow. For five minutes she rested with Kevin and two of the others on a wide ledge, passing around chocolate and raisins to revive their strength. Then she was up and moving again, always pushing, more and more of the cliff behind her.

Ahead scattered cheers pierced the stillness, but Shelley was in no hurry to reach the peak. Matching her strength to the mountain's challenge, she felt complete, as though a missing piece of herself had been restored at last. Once she had been convinced that this part of her life was closed forever. But here she was, climbing again.

Then her left boot suddenly jarred loose a shower of pebbles, abruptly ending her daydream. The stone that had been solid under her foot a moment earlier crumbled away and clattered into the abyss. Stomach churning, she felt the rock slither away from her hands. Anchored in a crevice above her, the rope snapped taut, and she swung suspended, clawing for a hold as the hungry chasm yawned beneath her.

A jutting rock grazed her cheek, but to her desperate hands the wall was blank and hostile. The mountain gave its secret, mocking laugh. How dare a weak, insignificant human defy its mysteries?

"Shelley!" Kevin cried. "Your rope'll hold you, you're OK—"

Even as he spoke her left hand clutched a rough outcropping of rock. Her arms took her weight again, and the rope fell slack. She hung there panting and sweating, as her feet sought out new holds.

"You all right?" Kevin asked. "You want to rest?"

"No, I'm fine," she said, fighting to catch her breath. She forced a ragged laugh. "This rope's tested for seven falls. That was number three."

"You're in good company. Cheryl fell before we even got to the cliff, remember? And Terry took a real good dive up ahead about five minutes ago."

Kevin's words took away some of the sting of failure. But Shelley's arms ached, her breath came in jerks. A wave of numbing weariness engulfed her. "I'll never make it," she groaned. "My hands are so cut up I can't hang on anymore."

"Mine, too," Kevin said. "We're almost there. Five more minutes and we'll be at the top."

She waited for a few moments until she was breathing easily again. Then she reached up and caught the next tiny niche in the cliff face. She was climbing once more, fiercely, up and up toward the summit.

The voices of the others drew closer and closer. "Enough here to make angels," she heard Cheryl exclaim and knew they were talking about the snow. The sun glinted on her face, but her hands were icy. Her left palm was scraped and bleeding, and she had torn the nail on her right thumb. Up to the next ledge, dig the right toe into another hole, wedge in a number six hexentric, and pull up with her arms, up, up—

A fresh burst of cheering broke out, somewhere just above her head. "This is it," Kevin called, and his voice rang with triumph. "The last boulder—I'm at the top!"

Something thudded against her helmet, and she thought he had kicked a stone loose, until she reached for her next hold and her fingers sank into a pocket of snow. "There's plenty more up here," Kevin announced. "Come on!"

Strong and firm, his hands grasped hers, and slowly she pulled herself to her knees. Then, miraculously, she was on her feet, enveloped by a cloud of applause.

"Hurrah, Shelley!" Voices clamored around her. "You did it!"

"There really is tons of snow up here!" she said, giggling and picking up a handful and tossing it like a clump of wet confetti. "Snow in July!"

"Shelley, congratulations." Steve took her

hand almost shyly. "I'm really proud of you, you know?"

For an instant, a twinge of anger and disgust marred the glow of victory for Shelley. *Now* that she had succeeded, he was proud of her, even though he had wanted to leave her behind.

But the moment was too precious to waste on resentment. "I loved it," she said. "Every minute of it—almost."

A few feet away a couple of girls had started a snowball fight. One of the boys began to argue with Steve: "Why should we plant a flag up here? Everybody leaves things up here, it trashes up the place."

Shelley took Kevin's arm, and together they stepped away from the chattering crowd. After the cliff face, the summit felt almost level at first. But within a few steps, Shelley realized the ground was sculpted into a maze of ridges, hummocks, and troughs, all treacherously slippery beneath the coverlet of snow.

"The mountain won't let us relax, will it?" she said. "Not even here."

"Nobody's walked on this snow before," Kevin told her. "We're leaving the first tracks."

"I should have been faster, getting up the cliff," Shelley reflected. "You had to keep waiting for me."

"You'll be faster next time," he assured her. "Probably you just need to get more confidence."

The wind wild against her face, the austere silence of the high, thin mountain air were working their old magic upon her, filling her with awe. For one aching moment, she longed to gaze at the panorama spread beneath her, the slopes they had just mastered, the cloud-shrouded peaks so close all around them. But even without the view, the mountain made her spirits soar. Far from the noise of the world below, beyond the pressures of civilization, she knew nature in all its power.

Yet Shelley knew that that time she felt something else, too—a blaze of happiness that had nothing to do with climbing Capital Peak. There would be a next time, she knew with a rush of certainty. She'd sign up for the next Climbing Club expedition. Now that she knew she could do it, she had no reason—no excuse—to stop. As she and Kevin stood side by side, alone in the mountain stillness, Kevin took her hand and pressed it between both of his. "I never thought this would really happen," he murmured. "I thought, when we had that argument that time, I thought after that I didn't have a chance."

"A chance?" she repeated. Her heart began to race, and it wasn't from the altitude.

"To see you again"—Kevin hesitated—"and to show you—to show you how I feel about you."

"Kevin?" She said his name in wonder as though she had never really heard it before. In his gentle grasp her hand was beginning to warm a little, and joy flooded through her.

"You never guessed?" he asked. "Not with

all those letters and phone calls and every-thing?"

"By the time I started to think about it, I figured I'd already ruined everything," she said slowly. "For a long time I was so afraid of losing Tom, I couldn't let myself care about anyone else. I kept insisting you and I were just friends. And then all I would let myself hope for was that we could save our friend-ship."

"Why do people say *just* friends?" Kevin demanded. "As if being friends didn't really count!"

"Or," Shelley added softly, "as if being friends couldn't turn into something even better."

"Well, it can," Kevin said. Then they were in each other's arms, alone together on the mountain, lost in a kiss that revealed all the secret dreams and hopes Shelley had hidden even from herself.

"Come on, folks!" Steve's shout echoed toward them on a gust of wind. "No time to hang around up here. We've got to get down to camp."

Slowly Shelley and Kevin pulled apart, un-til they were linked only by their clasped hands. But they lingered for a long moment, ignoring the sounds of the team readying for the descent.

"There's so much to say," Shelley blurted out. "I don't know where to begin—and now we've got to leave—"

"We'll have plenty of time," Kevin promised.

"It's not as if we can only be together on the top of a mountain, is it?"

"No," she said, laughing. "I guess not. There'll be a camp fire tonight and the drive back to Albuquerque tomorrow—"

"And Albuquerque's not all that far from Santa Fe," Kevin added. "I think from now on we'll be seeing each other quite a lot."

"Well, come on then," Shelley said. "We better go before they send a search party."

They turned together and headed back to join the others. Shelley listened to the soft *crunch-crunch* of their boots and knew that behind them they left a double trail of footprints across the fresh snow.